Justice at Red River

Benton was a quiet, peaceful town, at least until Witney Foran moved in. Then the rustling and the lynchings started, for Foran wanted to take over the whole territory. Backed by professional gunmen and the so-called bounty hunters who operated on the fringe of the law, he foresaw no trouble, for the sheriff of Benton was an ageing lawman, afraid to go against the gunmen.

There was but one seasoned gunfighter to lead the townsfolk in their stand against tyranny, but Condor, a man running from a past that threatened to catch up with him, was reluctant to start anything with Foran's gunslingers.

Then the Macey brothers bushwhacked Condor's best friend. Now it was time for him to buckle on his guns – and declare war.

Justice at Red River

PHILIP ASTON

A Black Horse Western

ROBERT HALE · LONDON

© 1971, 2002 John Glasby
First hardcover edition 2002
Originally published in paperback as
The Bounty Rider by Chuck Adams

ISBN 0 7090 7197 3

Robert Hale Limited
Clerkenwell House
Clerkenwell Green
London EC1R 0HT

The right of John Glasby
to be identified as author of this work has been
asserted by him in accordance with the Copyright,
Design and Patents Act 1988.

Typeset by
Derek Doyle & Associates, Liverpool.
Printed and bound in Great Britain by
Antony Rowe Limited, Wiltshire

1

Red River
Justice

At the full height of day the noon heat was brazen and oppressive. The sun glared from a blue-white sky and there was no shade around the tiny waterhole. The bushes were small, stunted growth, burned a deep brown and the rising walls of sand and rock formed a natural basin which caught and held the heat, refracting it from all sides, sending it pouring down in invisible, shimmering waves upon the two men lying in a shallow trench hollowed out by the vagaries of ages of wind and scouring sand.

For the better part of half an hour. the men had lain there, rifles thrust out in front of them, occasionally propping themselves up on their elbows, peering through the thin grass in an attempt to pick out movement on the hillocks all about them. In the sun's direct light, the results of the savage gun battle were pitilessly apparent. There was a deep red stain on Shorty Enwell's shirt where the blood still oozed from the bullet wound in his right shoulder in spite of the padding which his companion, Clem Foster had pressed against the hole. Groaning, Enwell flopped an arm across his eyes in an effort to ward off the blistering glare of the sun, then rolled over on to his side and presently, with a sluggishness that suggested the need of supreme concentration and effort, he pushed himself up on to his hands and knees, shaking his head slowly from side to side.

'Got to get out of here,' he mumbled. He tried to stand up, but couldn't make it and even as he fell forward on to his face, Foster reached out and grabbed his arm, pulling him down.

'They're still out there,' he hissed sharply. 'Keep your head down unless you want it blown off.'

'We can't stay here,' said the other hopelessly. 'Mebbe they have gone. Why'd they want to finish us off after they'd driven the steers away? They got no quarrel with us. We're just doin' a job here. We've no quarrel with Foran.'

'Everybody who isn't with him is against him,' muttered Foster grimly. 'He wants all of this territory for himself and he means to get it no matter how he does it.' He shifted his position on the scorching sand. striving to ease his body into a more comfortable posture. The sweat, streaming into his eyes, was blinding him and there was a long bullet burn along his left arm which stung where the irritating grains of sand had worked their way into the torn flesh.

'If I don't get to a doctor soon I won't be makin' it anywhere,' was the hoarsely mumbled response. Enwell opened his shirt carefully and examined the bleeding wound, gritting his teeth as each movement, however slight, sent a stab of agony lancing through his ravaged body.

'Not a chance.' Foster scrutinised the rising mounds around the waterhole, eyes screwed up into mere slits against the biting sunglare. 'Mebbe once it gets dark, we can risk it. But if we tried now, they'd pick us off the minute we showed our heads over those crests.'

'I don't think I can last out until dark.' The other laid his head weakly on his outstretched arm and closed his eyes.

Foster turned his head sharply. stared down at his companion. For a moment he felt sure the other was unconscious, possibly dead. Then he noticed the slow rise and fall of his chest, let the breath go in a soft exhalation. Damn it all, he thought angrily, fiercely; what had they done to deserve this? They had worked for Carson now for almost a year since they had ridden in together from Texas, looking for work, any kind of work so long as it was with cattle. That was really all they knew and when they had come upon this place, it seemed they had really dropped on their feet. The ranchers were all extending their holdings, building up their herds, driving them once every year to the railhead at Forbes Crossing, fifty miles to the east. There had been no sign of trouble then, no indication that a range war might flare up without warning.

Then Witney Foran had arrived in town. A hard-bitten and uncompassionate man, he had wasted no time buying land and building up a cattle empire which had grown rapidly over the months. As time had gone by, he had brought in men to enforce his will on the neighbouring ranchers. Within months, the peaceful valley had approached the brink of a full scale range war. Stolen cows found their way into the Double Circle herd which now numbered several thousand head. At least half a dozen men had been bushwhacked in the last few months and now it looked as though there would soon be two more.

The flat crack of a Winchester echoed across the inhospitable country and Foster dropped fiat, pressing his body tightly against the scorching sand. He had already noticed the strike of the slug to one side of him and the angry whine of the shrieking ricochet filled his ears. Narrowing his eyes, he studied the line of crests above him, knowing it would be useless to try to move into any better cover. There was just bare ground all about him.

As the afternoon wore on, the heat became fiercer and Foster noticed that his partner was now only partly conscious. He had lost plenty of blood; the wide stain on his shirt front testified to that and now and again, he would twist and jerk spasmodically on the ground, moaning through tightly-clenched teeth, his eyes rolling whitely in his head. Above the waterhole, the buzzards wheeled against the glaring sun, not daring to descend any further while there was still any sign of life below.

Weakly, Foster wiped the streaming sweat from his eyes and face, ran a parched tongue around equally dry, cracked lips. They had long since drunk the last of their water and there are limits beyond which human endurance cannot be pushed. The shimmering sand, the dizzying waves of heat were blinding him and when he saw the slight movement on the crest, he had only sufficient strength to lift the Colt and squeeze off a single shot.

One of the advancing men clutched at his stomach and reeled back, dropping in his tracks. Another, leaping down into the hollow, pointed the barrel of his Winchester at Foster's temple, finger tightening on the trigger. Another moment and he would have shot the man through the head, but at that instant, a harsh shout drew him back.

'Hold it, Frisco. I want these two alive.' Blackie Carron, Witney Foran's foreman, came forward, stood with legs braced, staring down at the two wounded men. 'Bring their horses here and put them on. We're takin' them back into Benton.'

'This one jest shot Clem,' grunted Frisco. 'You jest figurin' on tossin' 'em into jail?'

Carron grinned wolfishly. 'You got it all wrong, Frisco. These *hombres* have got to be a warning to anybody else who wants to try and stop Foran. The boss wants 'em taken in so we can string 'em up from a convenient tree.'

Frisco's eyes narrowed a shade. 'You reckon that the sheriff is goin' to allow that?'

One of the nearby men laughed harshly. 'You hear that! You ain't scared of Talbot, are you, Frisco?'

The other swung sharply at the scorn in the man's words. For a split second his right hand hovered close to the butt of the Colt in his belt, fingers clawed. He was a whiplash of a man, a born killer, fast with a gun, scarred by trouble and always looking for trouble. Restless and narrow of mind governed by passion, he killed for the sheer savage delight of it.

'All right,' snapped Carron. He stepped forward between the two men. 'I want no shootin' between ourselves. Now get their horses. We don't have all day to spend in this hell-hole. We've waited long enough in this goddamn blistering sun for my likin'.'

Slowly, Frisco relaxed, but there was still the look of murder in his black eyes, narrowed down to mere pinpoints. He glanced aside at the big foreman and a thought passed between them. Then he squared himself. 'I ain't scared of anybody,' he said ominously to the man who had spoken. 'You'd do well to remember that.'

'Hell, I didn't mean anythin',' grunted the other sullenly. He turned on his heel and ploughed his way through the shifting sand to the top of the nearby hillock. Ten minutes later, they had all mounted up and the column moved out, finding it difficult to control the two horses carrying the badly-wounded men. The animals could scent the nearness of death and they did not like it.

Shortly before five o'clock, the Double Circle riders tied their mounts in front of the jail, climbed down and started in a bunch for the front steps, walking slowly with the stiffness of all day in the hot sun and the saddle. On the boardwalk, Frisco stopped, glanced round at Carron. 'Reckon me and the boys have earned ourselves a drink, Blackie,' he said softly. 'I figure you can handle the rest of this.' There was a touch of insolence in his tone which the big foreman noticed instantly.

For a moment, a surge of anger seared through

Carron's body, then he caught himself. He had recognized Frisco's type the day the other had arrived at the Double Circle ranch asking for a job; a man who preferred more work with the gun than with cattle. A born killer, bucking for his job, ingratiating himself with Foran. Both men were of the same breed, tough and utterly ruthless. He guessed that Frisco was deliberately trying to rile him, hoping to make him go for his gun.

Forcing his anger down, he gave a terse nod. 'I reckon you're right, Frisco. Wait for me in the saloon. This won't take long. Once I get these two *hombres* locked up, I'll be over and we can plan the next move.'

He stood and watched the crew as they made their way across the dusty street, then stepped inside the sheriff's office, closing the door loudly behind him.

Ed Talbot swung his legs off the top of the desk and sat bolt upright in his chair, staring quizzically at the other, then knocked the length of grey ash off the end of his cigar and motioned Carron to a seat. 'Something on your mind, Mackie?'

'Plenty.'

The other raised his brows a little. 'What is it this time? More trouble with Carson's men?' There was a dispirited note in his deep voice. Suddenly, he began to feel all of his fifty-seven years. Being sheriff of Benton now was far different to the life it had been only a couple of years ago, he reflected. Then there had been very little trouble. A couple of drunks to lock up on a Friday night after they had been celebrating a little too heartily, sobering them up in the jail before letting them go on the Monday with a warning. He felt dead beat. This job was getting beyond his capabilities now, but there was nobody else who would take it on.

'I've got a couple of rustlers out there, Sheriff,' said Carron thinly. 'We caught them on Double Circle land with some of our beef. I want 'em both locked up until

Mister Foran gets here. Guess he has his own ways of dealin' with these rattlers.'

'All right. Bring 'em in.' Talbot got heavily to his feet and reached for the bunch of keys behind his desk.

Carron stood up, moved to the door, then looked back. 'I forgot to mention one thing, Sheriff. We had to put some lead into both of 'em. Guess you'll have to help me carry 'em in.'

Talbot looked on the other with a kind of impersonal interest, then followed him out into the street. Sighting the two men lying over their saddles, he stopped indecisively in his tracks, watching Carron with his baulked glance. 'But these men are dead,' he said sharply.

'Nearly – but not quite.' The foreman's tone was callous. 'They soon will be once Foran gets into town.'

Something in his tone checked the angry retort that leapt to Talbot's lips. In his violent years in the west, more than twenty years before, he had seen many iron-willed men such as Carron and he could sense the danger that lay deep in the other. Grumbling a little under his breath, he helped the other to lift the badly wounded men from the horses and carry them inside.

'You sure you want 'em locked in the cells?' he muttered hoarsely. 'They don't look to me as if they'll cause any trouble, not in their condition.'

'Lock 'em up, I said!'

For a moment, Talbot glared at the other, then his glance slid away and he sighed inwardly. 'At least I could get Doc Fortune to take a look at 'em. That ain't askin' much.'

Carron shrugged disinterestedly. 'Suit yourself about that, Sheriff. I daresay if he was to bind those wounds up a little, they might know who was hangin' them – and why. Reckon we've got to make an example of these critters if we're to stop this rustlin'.'

He waited until the two men had been laid on the low

bunks inside one of the cells and the door locked, then left the jail and made his way across to the saloon. Frisco saw him come in and drifted across from the bar. There was the same wolfish grin on his lean features.

'Everythin' go OK?' he asked.

Carron nodded. 'They're in one of the cells right now.' He turned away, motioned to one of the other men. 'Ride out to the ranch and let the boss know what's happened. I don't want word of this to get to Carson before we're ready.'

He went to the saloon door with the man, paused on the boardwalk, said in a low voice, 'Tell him what we've figured out. I reckon he'll agree. Might get him here a little quicker.'

The other nodded, moved over to his horse, climbed up into the saddle and spurred the gelding out of town. Carron watched him go, the white dust settling slowly behind him. Then he stepped back into the saloon, noticing as he did so the portly figure of Doc Fortune hurrying into the jail. Smiling a little to himself, he let the doors swing shut and moved over to the bar.

It had been a quiet evening in the Fast Gun saloon. Blackie Carron, smoking a thin quirley to pass the time, had remained seated at one of the tables, taking no part in the poker game going on among the rest of the men. Then, a little after nine, the doors of the saloon creaked open to let in Witney Foran.

The big rancher let his gaze travel around the room for a few moments before he walked across to the table at which his foreman sat and lowered himself into the chair opposite. 'I got your message,' he said curtly. 'You sure Carson knows nothing of this?'

'Don't see how he could, unless he's worried about his two boys and sent somebody to see why they haven't got back yet. Even then he won't know what really happened.'

'You have any trouble with Talbot?'

'Nothing I couldn't handle. He didn't like lockin' them away, but I reckon he knows better than to argue. Doc Fortune went in a while ago to fix 'em up a little. I figured they might as well know why they're bein' strung up when the time comes.'

Foran nodded his head slowly, his eyes shadowed in speculative thought, pinched a little to hide all that lay behind them. Taking out a cheroot, he lit it and let out a mouthful of smoke. 'I've had this thing figured out for some little time now, just waiting for things to play into my hands. Guess things couldn't have been timed better. Everything is perfect. You sure you've got everything attended to with no loose ends flapping about? I don't want a full-scale fight with Carson and the others until I'm good and ready – and that'll be when the Macey brothers get here. When that happens, we can ride roughshod over everybody in Benton. Right now, I just want to be sure that this is all inside the law' – he grinned viciously – 'even if we have to bend the law a little to suit our needs.'

'I don't see Talbot makin' any trouble,' grunted Carron. 'As for the rest, they're like sheep. They know better than to step into any trouble that isn't of their own making.'

'Maybe so.' Foran drew deeply on the cheroot. 'Better get Judge Fentry over and a couple of the Council. We'll make this real nice and legal.'

Blackie nodded, his dark eyes which seldom gave any hint of the workings of the mind behind them, glinting with a feral sheen. 'I'll have 'em across in ten minutes,' he promised.

He returned presently with the three men. Fentry looked uneasy when he spotted Foran, licked his lips nervously as Carron hustled him across to the rancher's table. His gaze flicked once in the direction of the Double Circle crew still engaged in their game of poker, then he glanced back at Foran.

'May I ask what is so important that you have to drag us across here at this time of night?' he asked.

Foran regarded him steadily for a long moment until the other lowered his eyes, then he said: 'I want you here to see that the trial we're just about to hold is perfectly legal.'

'Trial?' Fentry looked surprised. 'I've heard of no impending trial.'

'You wouldn't. The crime wasn't committed until today.' Foran sat back in his chair, perfectly composed. He nodded towards Carron. 'My foreman here and some of the crew came on a couple of Carson's men running beef off my range. There was a gunfight and one of my men was killed. The two rustlers were shot, but they're still alive and locked up in the jail across the street. We're going to try them on a charge of murder and rustling, right here and now. Once they've been found guilty according to the law, we intend to take them both out of jail at dawn and string them up as a warning to any others.'

Fentry turned his head slowly, looking around the saloon. 'I don't see the accused men here.'

Foran shook his head. 'Like I said, Judge. They were both wounded in the gunfight. Too badly wounded to be moved, I'm afraid.'

'But you can't try men in their absence like that. They have to be given a chance to defend themselves,' protested the other. 'If you don't do that, then you're going to be nothing better than a lynch mob.'

'You'll hear all of the evidence from my foreman and the men with him,' and Foran harshly. 'Now pick yourself a seat and we'll get on with it.'

Fentry made to answer, then thought better of it and sat down at the nearby table. The other two members of the Council, Steadman and Mendall, controlled their dislike of the proceedings, but with an effort, and joined him.

'All right,' Foran said pompously. 'This is an open and

shut case as I see it. Blackie here trailed some of my beef which had gone missing last night. Reckon those two *hombres* were driving 'em by a roundabout route because the boys here caught up with 'em at one of the dried-up waterholes on the perimeter of the spread where it borders the Badlands. That right, Blackie?'

'That's right, boss,' affirmed the foreman. He tossed back his drink. 'They elected to fight rather than surrender.'

'We only have your word for that,' Fentry said. He drummed with his fingertips on top of the table.

'You callin' me a liar, Fentry?'

'No. All I'm saying is that we've got two men's lives at stake here and it seems to me that we're only going to hear one side of this story. Could be that Phil Carson might claim that beef was his. That would put a very different light on the whole thing.'

'You think I don't know my own brand, Fentry?' Foran's eyes had narrowed down to mere slits. 'I say those cattle were mine and those two men in jail are rustlers. They also shot one of my boys in cold blood. You've heard what Blackie said. They were caught red-handed running the beef off my land. If those had been Carson's cattle they'd have stopped and let the boys check. As it is, they went under cover and opened fire.'

'I'd like to hear what Carson has to say about this before I make up my mind about it.'

'I'm not wasting any time getting Carson here.' Foran brought his clenched fist down hard on the table. 'We've got to have law here and from the way Talbot has been handling it so far, with kid gloves, there soon won't be any law and order at all. Once these then think they can get away with rustling my beef, they'll go on doing it. I don't want to have to bring in a bunch of hardened gunslingers to protect my interests, I'd sooner the law took care of them for me. But if it won't, then I guess I'll have to go about protecting my land and cattle in my own way.'

Fentry looked serious. Steadman coughed nervously, fiddled with his coat. Finally, he said: 'I see your point, Mister Foran. The only thing we all want to be quite clear on, I think, is that there's no danger of a mistake having been made. It's very easy, in the heat of the moment to—'

'Gentlemen,' Foran said sharply. 'Let's stop talking a lot of nonsense. I didn't come here to be lectured on how to run my own business. All I want to see is an example made of these two murderers. Now either you see it my way, or I do this on my own.' His tone became more ominous. 'I feel sure all three of you have sufficient regard to your own interests to know that I can make a good friend, but a very bad enemy.' He glanced at Steadman and Mendall, the two bankers, as he went on: 'I understand that at the moment, most of the other ranchers have credit notes with you which haven't been paid because of the drought. My own account is the largest you have, accounting for almost seventy per cent of your assets. If I were to take my business elsewhere, to Forbes Crossing, perhaps—' He let the rest of the sentence go unsaid, but the veiled threat was not lost on the two men who flanked Fentry.

Mendall hesitated for a moment, then gave a quick nod. 'I'm inclined to go along with you, Foran. Most of this may be circumstantial evidence as far as this court is concerned – I presume we are acting as a court of law here – but nevertheless, in view of the testimony of your foreman, it seems sufficiently strong to warrant a verdict of guilty.'

Steadman concurred with a brief nod of his head. He did not look up to meet Foran's satisfied glance.

'And you, Fentry. What's your opinion on their guilt?'

The judge ignored the implied sarcasm in the rancher's tone. He sat slouched in his chair, shoulders hunched forward. Eventually, he muttered: 'I want it to go on record that I'm not entirely convinced of their guilt, particularly since neither man has been afforded his right to speak for himself. We're bound by the laws of the United States here in Benton as anywhere else. One of them is that a man is innocent until he's proven guilty and that he has the inalienable right to speak on his own behalf. It seems that we've denied both of these men that right.'

'Nice talk;' muttered Frisco from the next table. He swung in his chair to face the judge. 'But we didn't come here for talk. Those two killers stretch a rope tomorrow at first light.'

'So you're had your minds made up about them all along. You only wanted me here to make things look legal. You never intended to give either of them a fair trial.'

Frisco got swiftly to his feet. 'All right, Judge. You've had your say.' The expression on his thin features was vicious and the older man shrank back from him. 'Now just do as you're told and there'll be no trouble. Otherwise—' He left the rest of his threat unsaid.

Foran grinned, picked up his unfinished drink, looked at Judge Fentry over the rim of the glass; a cold, appraising look. 'You heard what Frisco said, Judge. Now I advise you to go home and forget all about this. If there are any questions, particularly from Carson, I think you'll know exactly what to tell him.'

Fentry rose slowly to his feet, face tight. He paused for a moment beside Foran's table, then shrugged his stooping shoulders resignedly and made for the door. Outside, he sucked in a breath of air, held it for a moment as if it could, in some way, rid him of the smell of stale tobacco smoke and whiskey which had pervaded the saloon. The street was dark except for a light in the sheriff's office just across the road. Acting on impulse, he went over, feet shuffling a little in the dust.

Talbot was lying back in the big chair behind the desk,

his hat tilted forward over his eyes as he pushed open the door and went inside. The sound of the creaking, rusty hinges, slight though it was, brought the sheriff instantly upright, booted heels clattering on the floor. He seemed nervous and jumpy.

'It's only me, Ed,' Fentry said quietly. 'I've just been over at the saloon. Foran's there getting ready for a lynching in the morning.'

Talbot sighed heavily. He looked suddenly old. 'That's what I was afraid of,' he muttered. 'I figured that was in their minds when they brought these two riders in.'

'Foran was saying they'd been wounded in a gunfight.'

'That's right. Pretty badly wounded. They'd both lost quite a lot of blood and one's got a slug in his chest. They're both going to die anyway, but I suppose Foran can't wait for that to happen, he's got to hurry things on a little.'

'I gather that Phil Carson doesn't know two of his boys are here.' Fentry sat down wearily in the chair facing the desk. He stretched his legs out in front of him. 'Wonder if somebody shouldn't ride out and tell him. Maybe he'd want to do something about it.'

Talbot opened a drawer of his desk, took out a half-empty bottle and a couple of glasses. He poured a couple of glassfuls. 'I've been doing a lot of thinking about this, Judge. You know what would happen if Phil did get to hear tonight?'

Fentry sipped his drink, then nodded heavily. 'He'd bring some of his boys into town and bust these two men out of jail. Reckon a lot of innocent people might get hurt.'

'That's the way I figure it. On the other hand, if he didn't get to know until it was too late, I reckon he might think twice about it. After all, he wouldn't be able to bring 'em back.'

Fentry leaned forward, put his weight on his elbows, but

he only felt a slight pressure. There was a curious numbness in his body. I must be getting old, he thought bitterly, to sit here and let two men be lynched and do nothing about it. Fifteen, maybe ten, years ago, he'd have fought tooth and nail to prevent an injustice like this from happening. But since then so much had happened to dampen his spirit until now it had been put out altogether.

Talbot said, from a long distance, 'How much longer are we going to stand by and let Foran run this town just as he likes? He rides in here and starts to take over – slowly at first, until he's built up a private army of professional killers at his back – until soon, if we aren't careful, he'll own everything and everybody. If only the other ranchers would just wake up to the danger, band together, and fight. But we can't expect any miracles now. They're all watching out for themselves. Can't blame 'em, I suppose. We had everything peaceful until Foran came into the territory. None of the crews around here are professional gunmen like those riding with Foran.'

'We've got Condor,' Fentry said suddenly. He looked at the sheriff with some care.

'No good.' Talbot shook his head. 'He's a funny one, Frank Condor. A fast man with a gun, I'll admit that and if only half of the stories they tell about him are true, he could outdraw any of Foran's hired killers. But there's been something in his past, something he's running away from, that he never talks about. Nobody knows what it is, but it's enough to make him shut himself away from this business.'

Fentry pressed his lips together into a tight, determined line. He got to his feet. 'I think I'll go and have a talk with him, anyway.'

'There has to be something we can do to stop this,' Fentry said. He was watching Frank Condor who was sitting at the table in the dining-room of the small hotel, finishing his supper. 'If we don't, then we can say goodbye to law and order in Benton and no decent, self-respecting citizen will be able to walk down that street out there in safety. Believe me, I know what happens in a frontier town hike this when somebody as ruthless as Witney Foran rides in to take over.'

'But why are you telling me all this?' Condor eyed the other levelly across the table.

'I thought you might help us. Two badly wounded men are in jail right now and Foran means to have them taken out at dawn and hanged.'

'And you want me to go out there and stop it?'

Fentry shook his head. 'I've already given up all hope of that. Nothing is going to stop this lynching. But if it brings people to their senses and if they can get somebody to lead them, I'm sure all of the ranchers will band together to fight Foran.'

Condor drank down the hot coffee. 'If you're lookin' to me to lead them in this range war, then the answer's no. I've had enough of violence to last me a lifetime. I've seen what it can lead to and I want no more of it.' His tone was hard, emphatic. Bitter too. 'I've seen too many men die by the gun. Good and bad. I came here to get away from all that.'

'If things go on as they are doing, you won't be able to stay out of it.' Disappointment edged the other's tone. 'Foran won't stop with hanging these two men. This is just a gesture to let the other ranchers know that he means to be boss. I've seen this coming for more than a year now. The smaller men being squeezed out, mortgages called on as soon as their notes come up. Both Steadman and Mendall are in cahoots with Foran. Whether they're doing it because they like it or because they have no other choice, I don't know. But the outcome is the same whichever way it is. Men forced to sell their livelihoods for less than half of what their land and herds are worth. If they try to make a stand the ranches are burnt, cattle rustled, crewmen shot from ambush or called in the saloon. Where it is going to stop?'

'Seems to me you've brought a lot of it on yourselves. If you'd made your stand a year ago, you wouldn't be in this position.'

'I'm afraid it's always easy to be wise after the event.' Fentry sat silent for several minutes engrossed in his own bitter thoughts. When the big man facing him made no further attempt to speak, he said finally: 'I suppose I was wrong to think you might be prepared to help the town fight this menace. I don't know what has happened to make you like this. Maybe it's none of my business, but—'

'That's right, Judge,' interrupted Condor bitingly. 'It is none of your business.'

Fentry gave a harsh, brittle laugh. 'I've heard a lot of things about you, Condor. Some of them I frankly didn't believe, others I figured might just be true. They say you used to be some kind of marshal, down on the Texas border; a straight-shooting lawman with a fast gun. They reckon you even outshot Billy the Kid and locked him up once. If any of that's true. I can't figure why you should be content to stand by and see all of the injustice that's going on here in Benton.'

Condor's eyes turned blacker, his face shadowed. 'Better forget about me, Judge. I can't help any,' he said flatly.

For a moment another retort trembled on Judge Fentry's lips. Then he swung abruptly on his heel and walked quickly out of the dining-room. Condor continued to drink his coffee in the sudden brooding stillness. The street outside was equally quiet except for the faint murmur of sound that came from the Fast Gun saloon at the other end of town. At the moment, all he wanted to do was go along there and get drunk. At twenty-seven, he was a tall, lean man, face burned deep brown by long exposure to sun and wind; a man used to the long trails and hills. As he sat there a sharp feeling ran through him. It had been Fentry's last phrase which now turned its knife point in his mind.

He knew that some of his reputation had followed him here, had known it for a long time, just as he had seen this trouble looming up ever since Foran had moved in. Maybe, he reflected bitterly, he had also known that, sooner or later, somebody would put to him the same proposition that Judge Fentry had a few moments earlier and he had known, even then, what his answer would have to be. Sighing, he finished his coffee, rose to his feet, went up the creaking stairs to his room.

Without putting a match to the lamp, he went over to the window, staring down into the street outside. A cloud snuffed out the moon, but a moment later it returned, throwing an eerie light over everything. A light still showed in the sheriff's office and on the other side of the street, gleaming silver in the moonlight, more lights flared from the windows of the saloon. This trouble was the town's burden, he told himself; not his. Yet as he stood there, he had the feeling that his past was catching up on him fast and the thought of it burned away all of the warmth from his body. Going over to the small bureau beside the bed, he opened the top drawer, ran his fingers over the cold metal of the twin Colts which reposed there, the butts smooth with long use, the barrels and mechanism still slick with a faint sheen of oil. He had put them there on his first day in Benton, firmly resolved never to buckle them on and use them ever again.

Almost savagely, as if bitten by a rattler, he withdrew his hand, thrust the drawer shut with an angry motion. He had his own burden to bear. A burden which had turned a once simple world and existence into something of unguessed shadowed shades that demanded answers and haunted his dreams.

2

Lynch Law
Talbot

Talbot had slept for a little while and when he wakened
it was nearly dawn, with the slightest indication of grey
filtering through the dusty window panes. He got
abruptly to his feet, straightening his stiff limbs. Lighting
a cigarette, he walked around the desk. There was a dull
throbbing in his head, shooting through to his eyes. The
cigarette smoke removed some of the sour taste from his
mouth and now he was beginning to remember more of
what had happened the previous night. Then everything
came to him suddenly and his mind was not fully ready
for it. The shock of Foran's threat stiffened his body and
then left him limp the next moment. Hurrying over to
the street door, he opened it a crack and peered out. The
street was silent, deserted. No sign of any impending
trouble.

As his body began to tense again he tried very hard to
remain calm. Maybe it had just been a threat and nothing
more. After all, Foran would gain nothing by hanging two
badly wounded men. Scarcely had the thought crossed his
mind than the doors of the saloon opposite swung open
and three men stepped out on to the boardwalk. He saw

24

them glance over towards the jail, had time to notice that Witney Foran was one of them, before he stepped sharply back into the office, closing the door swiftly.

There was a stock of rifles locked in the cupboard on the wall and for a moment he debated the wisdom of getting one out and trying to stop these men. He had the key in his hand when the door was thrust violently open and Foran came into the office, with Blackie Carron and Frisco behind him.

Foran said with a deceptive softness: 'You thinking of breaking out some of those guns, Ed?'

Talbot stood facing the other, feeling foolish. He saw the sneering look on Frisco's smoothly handsome features, the right hand hovering close to the gun at his waist, then put the key back carefully on top of the desk.

Foran grinned broadly. 'That's better, Sheriff. Now you're showing some horse sense. Frisco's a little trigger-happy this morning. He's been up all night with the rest of us. We called a meeting to talk over the fate of those two prisoners you've got locked up in the cell. We reckon it's about time the representatives of Benton decided what to do with killers and rustlers. So we tried 'em both and found 'em guilty. Now we're here to carry out the sentence that was passed.'

'You've got no right at all to do this, Foran.' Talbot drew himself up to his full height. 'I'm the sheriff in town and I take my orders from Judge Fentry.' He looked from one man to the other. 'I don't see him here.'

'He was over at the saloon last night when we had the trial,' Blackie put in. 'Now just step on one side and don't make any trouble. We aim to get this thing over with fast. We don't have any time to waste talkin' with you.'

With an effort, Talbot fought to control the fear in his quaking mind. He knew he was bucking big trouble making a stand like this. None of these men would hesitate to shoot him, sheriff or not, but he felt that he had to make some kind of protest. 'I want to hear from Fentry about this before I turn those men over to you.'

Frisco said ominously: 'Reckon there'll be enough rope for you, Talbot, if that's the way you want it.'

'Now don't let's be like that, Frisco,' said Foran smoothly. His gaze never once left Talbot's face. 'I'm sure that the sheriff isn't so much of a fool that he doesn't recognize his position in this matter. He's paid to do as the law demands and if Fentry was here, he'd say the same thing.' His tone hardened a shade. 'Get the keys to the cells, Blackie. Talbot isn't going to do anything.'

There was a sudden change in the atmosphere inside the tiny office. It was as if every man there recognized that this was the final showdown. Talbot remained without moving for a long moment, then his shoulders slumped. He made to move back towards the desk but he didn't move quick enough for Frisco. Even as the sheriff steadied himself, the younger man's bunched fist lashed out. Blood spurted from the lawman's crushed nose as the blow connected. He staggered back with a bleating moan, put up a hand to his face, stared down incredulously at the wide smear of blood on the back of it.

Blackie had the keys by now. Swiftly, he moved towards the door at the rear of the office, opened it and went through. Foran said: 'Frisco. Go and help Blackie get those men out. Pity but we'll have to carry them out. I only hope they're sufficiently conscious to know what's going on – and why.'

Five minutes later, Enwell and Foster were carried out of the office and down the street. The rest of the Double Circle crew had already spilled out of the saloon and moved in a tightly-knit bunch behind them. Clutching his face, Talbot staggered after them.

The two men were taken to the big cottonwood that grew in the middle of the square. It was grey dawn now and there was activity in the street. Judge Fentry, who had not slept a wink that night, stood near his office door and watched the procession through veiled eyes. As they drew level with him, he turned deliberately, went inside the building and shut the door.

Out of the corner of his eye, Foran had noticed the other's actions. He tightened his lips. I shouldn't have allowed him to do that, he thought grimly. The day was coming soon when he would have to take care of the old fool. But now he was looking at the groups of townsfolk which had appeared on the boardwalks, attracted by the noise and activity. The more who came to watch, the better. By the time Carson and the others who were trying to stand in his way heard of this, they would realize he meant every word he said.

He strode to the head of his crew. 'All right, men. Get a couple of riatas over that limb. We've been up all night and it'll soon be sun-up.'

The ropes were brought and swung over the thick, out-jutting branch of the cottonwood. As the hempen rope struck Foster on the shoulder, he roused himself, seemed to realize what was happening, for his eyes widened in sudden shock, sweat standing out on his forehead, mouth twisting and working as if he was trying to say something.

Foran stepped forward. He stared down dispassionately into the other man's face. 'Reckon you've just got half a minute to say your prayers,' he said grimly.

Frisco came around, tightened the knot in the noose, adjusted it around Foster's neck. Foran jerked his head. 'Get that other *hombre* up too,' he ordered.

'Now see here, Foran.' Somehow, Ed Talbot had summoned up his courage. He came pushing his way forward, his face glistening with sweat just as Foster's was. 'You go through with this and you'll have every rancher in the territory up against you.'

'You really frighten me,' Foran retorted. He nodded to Frisco. The gunslinger moved forward, his eyes venomous.

'Reckon you ain't learned your lesson yet, old man,' he said thinly. Talbot made a move for his gun, but he was seconds slow. Frisco's fist lashed out. The lawman's gun was still half in its holster as the other hit him in the stomach, doubling him up with a sharp, explosive gasp of agony. Savagely, Frisco hit him again and again, driving him back against the railings; hard, punishing blows that left their mark on the unfortunate man. Desperately, futilely, Talbot attempted to fight back, his breath coming in hard, wheezing gasps. His vision was blurred by the blood which flowed into his eyes and against the superior speed and strength of the much younger man, he had no answer. Through the wavering haze of redness, he saw Frisco's sneering face, saw the other brace himself for the final blow, tried weakly to shift his body in an effort to ride the force of it. But the gunhawk had a tight grip on his shirt with his left hand, setting him up for the kill. The hamlike fist caught him flush on the face, hurling him back against the wooden railings, which splintered under his weight, throwing him into the dust. Even as he lay there, struggling to draw air into his aching, tortured lungs. Frisco was not satisfied with the effects of his beating. Drawing back his foot, he kicked the fallen man viciously in the small of the back. Pain jarred redly through the sheriff's body, lancing into his brain and, close behind it, came the blessed blackness of unconsciousness.

When he regained consciousness, his first impression was the awareness of pain. His body felt on fire and there was a sharp agony just above his kidneys. Weakly, he tried to lift himself, aware faintly of voices nearby. At first, they seemed far distant, so that he could not make out the words. Then, vaguely, he noticed the shadowy, blurred faces bending over him, opened his eyes wider.

'Just lie still, Sheriff,' said one of the voices. 'We'll soon have you fixed up.'

'Those two men,' he mumbled through swollen, bruised lips. 'What—' He shifted his gaze over Doc Fortune's shoulder, winced involuntarily as he caught a fragmentary glimpse of the two shapes which still dangled at the ends of the riatas. 'Guess it's happened,' he said dully. He pushed himself to his feet, holding on to the smashed railing for support, brushing off the doctor's hand. 'Ain't no reason to hold any inquest now.' He swallowed thickly. 'My only concern is what Carson will say when he hears about this.'

'Reckon you'll soon be able to find out,' Fortune said tightly. 'He's just riding into town now with a few of his men.'

Talbot's shaggy brows drew across his battered features as he stared along the street into the brightening sunlight. There was a buggy coming slowly down the main street, and behind it, half a dozen men, kicking up the white dust from under their horses' feet. He saw that the buggy was being driven by Atalanta Carson. Phil's daughter.

'She mustn't see this,' he mumbled thickly. Lurching forward, he tried to move towards the buggy, staggered and almost fell as the pain swept through his body and his legs turned to jelly. 'Hold up there,' Fortune said quietly. 'It's too late to do anything about it now. They're here.'

Talbot saw the look of horror that was stamped on the girl's face as she reined up hard. Phil Carson sat quite still for a moment beside his daughter, then got down stiffly and walked forward, his face suffused with a sudden anger. He threw a swift glance at the two bodies, then spun on Talbot. 'Who did this?' he grated harshly. 'I came here to report that Foster and Enwell hadn't showed up last night and I find – this.' He jerked a thumb towards the big cottonwood.

'Reckon you've got a right to feel angry, Phil,' Talbot said hoarsely. He fingered his bruised, bloodied face. 'I feel the same way, but there wasn't a thing I could do to stop them.'

'I asked you who it was.'

'It was Witney Foran and some of his gunhawks,' said Fortune thinly. 'They brought your two boys in yesterday afternoon. They'd both been shot and Foran claimed they were caught rustling some of his beef. He forced the sheriff to lock them both up, then they held a mock trial in the saloon during the night, found them both guilty and strung them up at first light.'

For a moment, Carson said nothing. He was a big, solid man whose convictions were as cold as ice. His eyes grew dark, still and in their depths a deep-seated wrath grew swiftly, kindling into a flame. 'And you all stood around and did nothing while he lynched two of my men.'

'I think it might be best not to be too hasty, father.' It was Atalanta who spoke. She seemed the more composed of the two now. Slowly, she climbed down from the buggy, looped the reins over the pole. 'From the look of the sheriff, I'd say he did everything he could to stop them.'

Carson stood quite still for a long moment, then he made a stiff gesture with his hand. 'I'm sorry, Ed.' He swung slowly, glancing at the townsfolk standing in little, silent groups on the boardwalks. 'I guess it's the town which is at fault.' There was naked scorn in his voice. 'Seems that Foran can come in here and ride roughshod over everybody and no one will lift a hand to stop him. Reckon it's about time someone did.'

Fortune sighed. 'You think that starting a range war is going to bring either of those men back, Phil?'

'Maybe not. But it'll let them rest easier.'

'You don't stand a chance against Foran's hired killers and you know it.' Fortune took the other by the arm. 'This is just what he wants you to do. You're the biggest of the ranchers around Benton. You don't have any note with the bank so he can't get at you that way. With the little men he doesn't have any trouble running them out of the territory and stealing their land and cattle. With you, he's got to try different tactics. That's the reason he did this. He knows your first reaction will be to declare war on him and he's ready for you.'

'I've got thirty good men who'll ride with me,' declared Carson stubbornly.

'Thirty men.' Fortune nodded. 'But how many of them can handle a gun like the killers he's got on his payroll, with more gunslingers riding in to join him every day? Come over to the saloon, Phil, I want to talk to you.' He turned to Talbot. 'In the meantime, you'd better go and clean yourself up, Sheriff. I'll come along in a little while and take a look at you.'

Fortune did not say anything more until he was seated at one of the tables in the saloon, with Phil Carson seated opposite him. Then he rummaged in his pockets, until he had brought out his pipe, thrusting the brown strands of tobacco into the bowl, firing it up and sucking the smoke deeply into his lungs. Over the smoke, he studied Carson. 'Like I said out there, Phil. You don't have a chance against Foran on your own. You rush into this thing with your eyes shut and driven only by anger, and he'll cut you and your crew into little pieces.'

Phil Carson did not move. His face might have been carved out of stone for all the emotion that showed on it now. Then, lowering his gaze, he stared moodily at the glass of whiskey in front of him.

'You're surely wise enough to see that I'm talking sense, Phil. If only we had seen this coming a year ago things could have been very different. We could have stopped Foran and run him out of the territory before he had a chance to build up his strength. But now he's too big for anyone to handle alone.'

'And you're saying that the others will come in with me and finish this thing?' Carson shook his head savagely. 'You know damn well they won't. They're too busy looking out for themselves.'

Fortune peered into the glowing bowl of his pipe, his face tight and serious. 'They might be prepared to do that if we were to find the right man to lead them.'

'To do that you'd need a man as fast and deadly with a gun as Frisco and the rest of that bunch of hired killers.'

'I know. I'm thinking about Frank Condor. They say he used to be a frontier marshal one time – about the fastest gun there was in North Texas. Now if he could only be persuaded to come in with us, we could get the backing of the others, band together, and force a showdown with Foran.'

Carson gave a hard, brittle, laugh. 'The Lord only knows where you got that idea from. I've been watchin' Condor ever since he arrived in town. He's a man with a past. He doesn't belong here and this town means nothin' to him. Could be he's got as much reason to hate it as Foran has. They may even be birds of the same feather for all we know.'

'Once a lawman, always a lawman,' put in Fortune sagely. 'At least it's worth a try.'

'No. I'll handle this my own way.' Carson finished his drink, pushed back his chair and got to his feet. 'You said only one thing I'd agreed with and that was we ought to have run Foran out of the territory a year ago. It may be too late now, but by God, I'm goin' to have a try. Those cattle he reckoned Foster and Enwell were runnin' off were mine. They were bringin' them back off Double Circle range. I know that for a fact because I gave them the chore to do.'

'And they're both dead now,' Fortune muttered harshly. 'And that's what will happen if you send any more of your men after Foran. He's got the gunhawks to do it.'

'I'll bear that in mind,' said the rancher sombrely. He moved past the doctor, paused, glanced down. 'Thanks for the drink, anyway, Doc.'

*

Slim Edmond had a smallish shack on the eastern edge of town with a wide view towards the distant hills. It sagged a little around the roof and was quite old like most other similar shacks on the outskirts of Benton. Many of these buildings were abandoned, had not been lived in for more than ten years, while others had been taken over, without vested titles, by the more independent citizens, made habitable where their occupants could remain unmolested and with the maximum of privacy. Slim rose and breakfasted late. It was a fine, still morning and already there was the promise of heat in the air. Stepping out into the yard, he threw a quick glance along the main street. It seemed peculiarly empty for that time of morning and he fell to wondering about this. Shortly after dawn, he had heard the sound of riders moving fast out of town, but he had thought nothing about it then. Now he began to consider it and when he saw the tall figure of Frank Condor walking quickly in his direction, he knew by the other's demeanour that there was something wrong. Even though he had known the other since Condor had arrived in town, probably knew him more intimately than anyone else in Benton, there were facets to this dark-eyed man which he felt he would never know or understand. There was a deep current that ran within Frank Condor which could not be fathomed by any man. Perhaps some day, a woman might do it, but even that was highly conjectural.

'Howdy, Frank,' he said as the other opened the gate and walked into the yard. 'You look like a man with all the worries of the world on his shoulders.'

Frank's face had shed its customary good-humoured expression, had now become sober and perhaps a little dangerous. He leaned against the nearby post and built himself a smoke, rolling the tobacco with expert fingers. Once it was lit, he said tonelessly: 'Two men were lynched this mornin', Slim. Foran and his boys strung them up from the cottonwood.'

'Two of Phil Carson's boys?' Slim's face was expressionless.

'That's right. How'd you know?'

'Reckon I've seen this comin' for a long time. Phil's spread is one of the biggest in the territory and he's the one man that Foran can't buy out. So he has to do things this way.' He cocked an inquisitive eye at Condor. 'You ain't thinkin' of sidin' up with Phil, are you?' He made it a hopeful question.

'I'm not thinkin' of sidin' up with anybody. I've already had Judge Fentry to see me, askin' me to side up with the ranchers and lead 'em against Foran.'

'And you don't cotton on to that idea?'

'I've finished fightin' other people's battles for 'em,' Frank replied. 'There comes a time when you reach a fork in the trail. Then you either go on in the old way, killin' and waitin' for the time when you bump into a man who's a shade faster than you are, or you turn off the trail at that point, put it all behind you and hide yourself away in some place where nobody knows you.'

'And that's what you're tryin' to do here in Benton.' Slim shook his grizzled head slowly. 'You can't do it, Frank. I guess I know you better than most. You won't stand by and see a man like Foran take over the town and drive all of these honest folk off their land by the law of the sixgun. If you did just stand by and watch that happen, then I figure there'd have to be a damn good reason.'

'Could be there is,' said Frank enigmatically. He did not look at the other as he spoke. 'My guns are locked away in a drawer in my room. I don't intend to fasten them on again.'

Slim was silent for a while. Presently, he said: 'I figure it may not be any of my business, but if it'll help to talk about it, I'm always ready to listen.'

Frank gave him a bright-sharp stare. 'There's nothin' much to talk about, Slim. You're imaginin' too much.'

'I can tell when a man is runnin' away from somethin' and nobody shucks their guns just like that. You've got somethin' eating at you and if you don't let it out, it's goin' to destroy you. Somethin' happen down Texas way? Somethin' you've been keepin' inside you for so long that it's made it impossible for you to see things straight?' He eyed Frank shrewdly. 'They say you were a good marshal once. Then you just threw up everythin', rode out of town and kept on ridin' over the hill. Don't make sense to me.'

'Quit riding me. Slim. I'm in no mood for it right now.'

'I'm danged if I will,' declared the oldster stubbornly. 'I don't like to see a good man go off on the wrong trail. What was it? You shoot an innocent man? It happens, even to the best lawman.'

A flicker of expression came to the other man's face and lit the back of the dark eyes. He laid his glance on Slim and it was like the edge of a knife, sharp and ready to cut. Then, softly, he said: 'He wasn't innocent, Slim. He was once a good man, but he turned killer. He rode with Quantrill and he didn't have his fill of killin'. So he had to team up with a bunch of outlaws. One day they rode into town and decided they'd hold up the bank. I called on him to throw down his gun and give himself up, but he drew first and I had to shoot him. There was no other way of stoppin' him. If I hadn't done it, he'd have ridden out and killed more innocent men before somebody else got him in the end.'

Slim's eyelids crept nearer, accentuating his shrewd expression. 'Who was he, Frank?' he inquired softly.

The answer was a long time in coming, so long that Slim began to think he would never get a reply. Then Frank said huskily: 'He was my brother, Slim.'

The older man stolidly accepted this information. He nodded his head. 'I can understand your feelings, but it's no good runnin' away. There are times when a man reaches the crossroads and has to take one turnin' or the other. I don't reckon it'll do any good for me to tell you I figure you did the only thing you could.'

'You think I haven't tried to tell myself that all this time?' Condor's voice still had the hard edge to it. 'What made him go that way and me go mine? He knew evil and I had sworn to fight it.'

'Life's a brutal thing,' Slim told him soberly. 'Full of torment for all of us. You've thought about this long enough. It's time to put it out of your mind for good. You can't go on carryin' this burden with you.' He jerked a thumb towards the door of the shack. 'I've got coffee on the stove, Frank. Come inside.'

Condor followed the other into the shack. There was a pot of coffee on the back edge of the iron range. Slim lifted a couple of cups down from the hooks, poured some out and pointed to the condensed milk and sugar. He continued to watch the other, puzzled and a little uncertain. 'I wish I'd known what was ridin' you all this time. Frank.'

'It wouldn't have helped, believe me.'

'Mebbe not' The other gulped his coffee. 'But with this trouble beatin' up all the time, it might have made you change your mind about a few things. Most of the folk around here are good, honest men. They don't have much truck with gunhawks like those ridin' for Foran. All they ask is to live and let live. Now Foran is threatenin' their very existence. If they don't fight, they'll all go under. Can't you see that?'

'Sure, I can see it. I've seen it one time too many for my likin'. That's why I don't want any more of it.'

Slim's face was grim. 'You can't run away from it this time, no matter how hard you try. You're part of this town whether you like it or not. You think that Witney Foran is goin' to leave you alone, just because you walk around without any guns? He's not that type. Just because a man isn't armed, it won't stop him havin' him gunned down if it suits his purpose.'

'Meanin' what, Slim?'

'Just this. Whether you like it or not, you've got a reputation as a fast gun. Foran knows that, so does Frisco. And there's been talk of more gunhawks ridin' in to join Foran. Sooner or later, one of these *hombres* is goin' to get it into his head that he'll be a real big man if he guns down Frank Condor, Texas Marshal.'

'And you think I ought not to tempt 'em?'

'I think if you wore your guns you might make 'em think twice about it.'

'Like I told Judge Fentry last night, I'll bear that in mind, Slim. He wanted me to lead the ranchers against Foran.' He finished the coffee, moved across the room doorward. Lifting the latch, he hesitated for only a second, then passed out of the shack.

By the time the sun was lifting towards its zenith, Frank Condor was approaching the rising rimrocks of the western plateau that bordered the Badlands on the edge of the Double Circle spread. After riding out of Benton, he had pushed his mount swiftly, hurrying along the final ridge of the steep drop-off. Reaching the rim, he paused, seeking the trail that led directly down towards the dense jack pine and manzanita. From this vantage point, he was able to look out over the vast stretch of country that lay in a great rolling plain below him. On either side of him, shimmering in the noon heat, there were razor-backed slopes that dropped away precipitously, where one miss-step on the part of horse or rider would mean instant and certain death.

Although his talk with Slim was urgent enough to make him restless and uneasy, it had not been enough to make him able to rid his mind of doubt. Far back in Freemount, after he had killed his brother, he had felt haste. A deep and urgent haste to get away from that town with all of its memories, to ride out on to a trail, any trail, and keep on riding, in an attempt to get so far away that he would be able to forget what he had done, would be able to sleep easy at night and wake to a new day without a care in the world. But so far, that had proved impossible. His past was for ever rising up and haunting him, riding him, driving him deeper and deeper into a morass from which there was no escape.

Because of this, he had been forced to sit by and watch the dark shadow of defeat and ruin settle over Benton and the people who lived there. It had not been easy to stand by and watch it happen, to know that he might have been able to stop it. Yet always, that memory had been strong enough to hold him back. Even now, he doubted his ability to go back to the old ways of violence, to living by the gun, even if it meant upholding the law in this town.

Touching spurs to the horse's flanks, he set it on the downward path which wound in and out through great boulders, now scarcely able to see his mount's head out in front of him, the slope was so steep. But the bay was sure-footed and he felt little concern about getting down safely. Half an hour later, he reached the lower ground where the trees grew thick about him. Here, he was out of sight of the main valley trail and he had progressed for almost half a mile before he heard the unmistakable tattoo of another rider close by. Reining up sharply, he eased the bay into the thick undergrowth and waited, listening to the other horse coming on. There was something about that sound which warned him instinctively of trouble. Whoever the rider was, he was pushing his mount hard at a punishing pace.

The drumming of hoofbeats drew level with him, still some distance away, so that he was unable to make out the rider, then began to draw away once more. Gigging his mount forward, he came out of the trees just in time to catch a glimpse of the rider. He felt a distinct shock of surprise when he saw that it was Atalanta Carson. For a moment, he stared after her, then swung in the saddle, and looked in the opposite direction. From where he was, he now had an unbroken view of the entire sweep of the wide valley and his eyes drew down into slits as he saw, on a far ridge, the small cloud of dust, no bigger than a man's hand, which betokened the presence of other riders, heading quickly in his direction.

So that was it. He could not make out the identity of those other riders, but he had little doubt they were some of Witney Foran's men. Without waiting, he spurred his bay down on to the wide trail and headed after the girl. By now, she was more than a mile ahead of him, riding fast, but it was soon evident that her mount was tiring rapidly. Clearly she knew that she was being closely pursued and it must have also been obvious to her that she had little chance of reaching her own spread before those men behind caught up with her. Savagely, he touched rowels to his horse's flanks, got some response from it as the bay gamely increased its speed. Slowly, the distance between the girl and himself narrowed but a quick glance over his shoulder showed him that the tightly-knit bunch of men were also gaining fast.

He had got to within a couple of hundred yards of the girl before she became aware of his presence. She must have caught the beat of his mount's hoofs above that of her own, for she turned her head quickly, caught a swift glimpse of him, then kicked desperately at her horse's flanks, forcing her deadbeat mount to expend the last of its rapidly failing energy in one wild dash, evidently believing him to be one of her pursuers.

Ahead of the girl was a narrow fringe of trees towards which she suddenly swung her mount. As she did so, he saw her make a grab for the rifle in the scabbard beside her. Whether it was this unwise move, or an unsuspected hole which threw the horse, he did not know; but the next second, her mount went down on to its forelegs, throwing

her from the saddle. She fell heavily and Frank slid apprehensively from the saddle and ran towards her, afraid that
the blow had stunned her, had possibly caused her far
worse injury. But as he came up to her, she made a grab
for the rifle which had fallen beside her, swung it and tried
to line up the barrel on his chest as he bent over her.
There was both fear and fury showing on her face.

Grasping the barrel, he slowly forced the rifle aside,
twisting it from her grasp. She sank back on to the ground,
heavily. Then her eyes widened a little as she recognized
who it was.

'Frank! Oh God, I nearly shot you.'

He grinned at the look of discomfiture on her features.
'Forget it, Atalanta. Guess it tells me you aren't too badly
hurt.'

'Just shook up. I think.' She eased herself to her knees,
then threw a swift look back along the trail. 'Foran's men!'
she said in a hoarse whisper. There was a faint tremor in
her voice. 'They jumped me on the edge of the spread.
Frisco is with them. He—'

'No time for explanations now, Atalanta. We've got to
figure a way out of here.'

'My horse is finished.' She pointed. 'And yours doesn't
look as though it could carry both of us. Those killers can't
be more than a mile away now. They'd overhaul us before
we could travel another mile.'

'Then we'll have to stand them off here.' He helped her
to her feet, hustled her into the brush. 'You got any shells
for this rifle?'

'In the saddle-bags.' She nodded towards the fallen
horse. Ducking low, Frank ran to the horse, grabbed the
bags and raced back. Already, the sounds of the approaching horses could be heard quite clearly. Crouching down
in the thick brush, he opened the saddle-bags and took
out the spare shells, laying them close beside him.

'Maybe they'll ride on by,' suggested the girl in a whisper. He shook his head emphatically.

'They'll spot that horse of yours even if he doesn't make a sound and give us away.' He tightened his lips into a thin, hard tine as he lifted the rifle, squinting along the sights. 'Besides, it's too late now. They're here.'

He saw the bunch of men ride around a tall knoll, then pause as Frisco, riding in the lead, suddenly spotted the injured horse and held up his hand. He could almost see the grin on the lean gunhawk's face as the other pushed his horse forward a little way.

'Better come on out of there, Atalanta,' Frisco called loudly. 'Or do you want me to have to come in and get you?'

'Come ahead it you like, Frisco,' Frank called sharply. 'But I'll put a bullet between your eyes if you do.'

The effect of his voice was instantaneous. Frisco leapt from his saddle and crouched down beside his horse, the rest of the Double Circle men doing likewise. There was a long pause, then Frisco's voice came back. 'That you, Condor?'

'That's right. Now saddle up and ride on out of here.'

Frisco's harsh, sneering laugh cut through the taut stillness. 'Hear that, boys. That tinhorn marshal wants us to leave.' He shouted scornfully. 'I've been hearing all about you, Condor – what a big man you are, and fast with a gun. I ain't seen you wearin' shootin' irons yet. Could be that all those stories were nothin' but a lot of hot air. You're just plain yeller, Condor.'

'Why don't you make your play and find out?' Raising himself a little on one elbow, Frank watched the scene carefully, ready for Frisco's first move. He knew the gunslinger was not the sort of man to waste time with talk, particularly since he must already know that there were only the two of them there, himself and the girl. That fact alone, must make Frisco pretty brave. Besides, he figured, Frisco would have been doing a lot of talking in the past and he now had to back that talk up with play in front of his own men.

The other made his move a few seconds later. A volley of shots crashed into the brush, tearing leaves and twigs down on to their heads. Under cover of the fire, Frisco jumped for the shelter of the nearby rocks, hurling himself out of sight among them, loosing off a couple of shots as he did so. Frank fired one shot after him, saw it chew dust off the rock behind which Frisco crouched. The rest of the Double Circle crew scattered, racing for cover.

Frank eased himself forward a little way and tensed. More shots erupted from among the rocks, but the dense brush shielded the girl and himself from view and he guessed the riders were aiming blind, hoping that if they pumped in sufficient shots, they were bound to hit something. Then Frisco yelled something in a high voice. The firing stopped. Pressing himself tightly against the ground, ignoring the sharp thorns which raked his exposed flesh, Frank wriggled towards the edge of the brush. There was not much sound now but that which filtered through to him was ominous. The slight noises were stealthy. The men were on foot and edging in from all sides, moving into the thicket from the sides and rear, ready for the kill.

Lying quite still now, Frank found that he was the focus of attention of the tiny brown heel-flies which were swarming around the tangled brush, a buzzing cloud of them at his face, alighting hungrily on the mass of scratches caused by the chaparral. He motioned the girl to remain hidden in the brush, wriggled further to one side, squinting into the harsh sunglare, striving to make out any movement among the rocks and distant bushes. Now the rifle was a distinct disadvantage. As a long range weapon it was ideal, but with the Double Circle men so close, a Colt would have been a far better weapon. Backing out a little way into the open he edged along a narrow game trail, then froze as he made out the swish of branches being eased aside by a moving body. The sound was dangerously close, a little to his left. Holding his breath, moving his gaze swiftly from side to side, he picked out the snap of a twig, muted a little by the cushion of decayed leaves underfoot.

Then there came other sounds on his right, the stealthy sounds of men working to a close pattern to hem him in. There was no doubt that Frisco was feeling pretty confident he had the girl and himself trapped, and not without good reason. Wiping the sweat and buzzing flies from his face, eyes smarting and stinging where they had bitten into his flesh, he paused, made out the slight movement ahead of him along the game trail. Propping himself up on one elbow, he levelled the rifle. One of the men was moving out of the brush towards the trail. A second later, the man stepped into view, caught sight of him in the same instant and swung up his Colt. The rifle hammered in Frank's grasp, spinning the man round. The lash of return fire came a split second later, but the other was already dead on his feet and the impact of lead in his body sent the slug whining off the rocks a couple of feet from Frank's head.

Another gun roared from behind, the slug head-high. Only the fact that he was crouched down saved Frank at that moment. He slammed a bullet in the direction of the hidden marksman, heard a faint yelp of pain as the lead found its mark.

A man's voice yelled: 'He's over here, Frisco. We've got him pinned down.'

A murderous pattern of bullets poured into the narrow trail where Frank had dropped as low as the chapparal would allow. All about him, the undergrowth was alive with the crashing of men, the need for stalking their quarry was gone now that his whereabouts had been pinpointed. He half-rose to his feet, made a blind run into a thicket, hoping to lead the men away from the girl. He had no idea why they wanted her so badly, but guessed it could not mean any good for her. Seconds later, he emerged into a small clearing, blundered forward a couple of paces, then stopped in his tracks as Frisco moved out from behind one of the trees, his gun levelled on Frank's chest.

'Now just hold it right there, Condor,' grinned the other viciously. 'I don't know why you had to horn in where you wasn't wanted, but seein' that you are here, I figure we'll just have to finish you off. Nobody'll find your body until the buzzards have picked it over.'

Frank fingered the useless rifle helplessly, wondering if he might just have the chance to lift it and squeeze off one shot. Then he saw the other's finger tighten on the trigger of the Colt, saw the knuckles whiten, and knew he didn't even have that chance.

A gun roared and he flinched instinctively, tightening the muscles of his stomach automatically, waiting for the leaden slam of the bullet striking in through flesh and bone. Through blurred vision, he saw Frisco spin, clutching at his right arm where blood was beginning to soak through the cloth of his shirt, the Colt dropping from nerveless fingers. For a moment, the killer stood motionless, then he whirled and plunged into the brush. Frank lifted the rifle, loosed off a single shot after the fleeing man, knew from the hurried sounds of retreat that the slug had missed its mark. Then he turned swiftly, saw Atalanta move out of the thicket behind him. There was a smoking Derringer in her hand. Thrusting it into her belt, she ran across to him.

'Are you all right, Frank?' she asked breathlessly.

He nodded. 'Just scratched by the thorns.' he replied. He cast about him anxiously, listening for the sounds of the other men converging on the small clearing. Then, grasping the girl's hand, he hustled her into the trees.

'Hurry! We may be able to reach their horses before they catch up with us. If we can grab a couple for ourselves

and spook the rest of them, we may get out of this mess
with whole skins.'

He rubbed at the maddening flies as he ran, peered
through stinging eyes at the game trail which wound away
in front of them. There was more rustling in the brush to
their left and it decided their direction. Motioning the girl
off the trail, they ran through dense brush where whiplike
branches slapped at their faces, slammed the backs of
their hands and arms as they held them up to their heads
in an attempt to ward off the vicious blows. Bullets were
chasing them all the way and in the intervals between the
gunblasts, he heard the yells of the men as they closed in.
Another open patch with a wider trail leading off to their
right. His face felt a tight mask of drying blood and a thousand fly stings. Beside him, the girl still ran, her breath
coming in hard, rasping gasps through trembling lips, but
she made no complaint at the punishing pace.

Their view through the branches and leaves was
restricted and they were forced to rely more on sound
than sight to estimate the position of the Double Circle
riders and how many were still on their trail. Then,
abruptly, the tangled undergrowth thinned. They were out
in the open with the sunlight blinding in their eyes, the
glare bouncing off the hard rocks, the heat striking at
their bodies with an almost physical force where it was
refracted off the rock in dizzying waves.

Now the rocks and the spiky cactus were the main
enemies. Their pursuers were still apparently tangled in
the impeding brush. Casting about him. Frank eyed the
rocks in an attempt to orientate himself, then pointed
with the rifle. 'That way,' he hissed urgently.

Stumbling, they clambered over a low, razor-backed
ridge, threw themselves down the far side as the yells
behind them grew louder. Less than a minute later, they
spotted the horses in a loose bunch. None of them wore
ground reins and Frank felt thankful for that. Those first

rifle shots had made the men jump for cover in a hurry, giving them no time to ensure that the horses were secure.

Frank felt his exhaustion then, a deep leaden weariness that descended upon his body. With a supreme effort, he caught the reins of the nearest horse, pulled himself up into the saddle, vaguely aware that the girl had done likewise. Jabbing spurs hard into the horse's flanks, he pulled round on the reins, at the same time firing a shot into the air. His mount leapt forward and in the same moment, the other horses scattered, racing out towards the desert, trailing their reins along the ground behind them. A flurry of shots sounded from the thicket and above the din, Frank made out the yell of Frisco's voice above the others.

'They're gettin' away! Grab those damned horses!'

Bending low over his mount's neck, he gave the animal its head, the girl racing alongside him. Not until they were well out of range of the Double Circle men did he ease up. They were out on the mesa now, having deliberately swung away from the main trail, for the going was easier here and there was no difficulty in picking their way through the scattered brush and stunted pine which dotted the area.

'Reckon we've lost 'em,' he said simply. 'They won't be able to catch those other horses for a while. Plenty of time for us to reach your Dad's spread.' He gave her a shrewd glance. 'Do you know why they were after you like that? Reckon they must've had some good reason.'

'I haven't the slightest idea. I was on my way back from town when I spotted them heading for the trail. I could tell by the way they were riding that they meant trouble and since that double lynching yesterday, I didn't wait to find out. I just rode, giving the horse its head.' She paused, bit her lip. 'I guess if you hadn't showed up, Frank, they'd have got me.'

Frank furrowed his forehead in sudden thought. It didn't make much sense on the face of things. It was well known that Witney Foran wanted Phil Carson's spread but somehow Frank had never considered it likely that Foran would declare war on women. It seemed more probable that this was some of Frisco's doing. He had always considered himself to have a way with the ladies. There was a very definite possibility that he had had his eye on Atalanta for some time and if she had spurned his advances, there was no telling what lengths he might go to. Frank himself had to admit that she was a very beautiful woman. He eyed her from the edge of his vision. Even after all she had been through, she still held herself proudly, tall and erect in the saddle. He saw the lovely curve of her throat, the wide-set eyes and the long hair which curled to her shoulders from beneath the wide-brimmed hat she wore. As if feeling his gaze on her, she turned her head, smiled a little.

'You look like a man with something on his mind, Frank,' she said disarmingly.

He shrugged. 'Nothin' in particular. Just wonderin' what Frisco had on his. Reckon it'd pay you to watch that snake, Atalanta.'

She nodded. 'I'll be ready the next time,' she said, and there was a note of confidence in her voice which surprised Frank.

They threaded their way through the descending bed of a ravine, edging their mounts around gigantic boulders washed down by some great river in a past geological age. On either side of them were great fissures in the rock with sharp, ragged ledges that overhung the narrow, winding trail. By the time the sun was lowering towards the western horizon, dipping down the long curve of the cloudless heavens, they came within sight of the valley that marked the perimeter of Carson's spread.

Twenty minutes riding and the ranch house came into sight, a long, brick and wood building, with a low sloping roof and several outbuildings ranged alongside it. There was a large corral in front of the wide courtyard and two men standing on the porch which ran along the front of the house, shaded from the direct light and heat of the sun by the overhanging roof. As they rode up, Frank recognized one of the men as Phil Carson. The other man was Judge Fentry.

Dismounting, he followed the girl across the dusty courtyard, aware that the two men were watching him with some surprise. He grew conscious of his own appearance, put up a hand to his scratched face.

Phil Carson threw a quick glance at the two horses standing in the courtyard, must have recognized them instantly as having the Double Circle brand, for he stepped down and came quickly towards them.

'What happened, Atalanta?' he asked, looking from the girl to Frank, then back again.

'Frisco and some of Foran's riders tried to take me, Dad,' she explained. 'They would have succeeded if it hadn't been for Frank. We managed to fight them off. I think one or two of them were killed and I shot Frisco myself.'

'You killed him?' There was a note of alarm in Judge Fentry's voice as he overheard this piece of information.

'Just put a piece of lead in his arm,' Frank put in. 'Reckon if she hadn't, I'd have been dead too. He had the drop on me.'

Carson nodded. He laid his severe gaze on Frank. 'I'm obliged to you for saving Atalanta, Condor,' he said harshly. 'I only wish I could say that this is the end of it. Unfortunately, from what the judge has told me, it's only the beginning.'

'I don't understand, Dad,' Atalanta looked from one man to the other. 'What do you mean?'

It was Judge Fentry who spoke, his voice serious. 'I've just come from town. I've known for some time that Foran has been hirin' men to back up his play. Frisco was one of the first of the gunslingers he brought into the territory. Shortly before noon, a couple more rode into Benton.' He glanced at Frank. 'Reckon you may have heard of 'em, Marshal.' He deliberately emphasized the last word. 'The Macey brothers.'

Frank stiffened. His face took on a hard, grim look, eyes narrowed down to mere slits. 'I've heard of 'em,' he said flatly, tonelessly.

'Figured you might have.' Fentry jerked his head in a quick nod. 'A couple of fast guns from south of the frontier. Somewhere down Texas way. You ever run into 'em?'

'Might have.' Frank's voice was non-committal. 'They been givin' you trouble in town, Judge?'

'There weren't any while I was there, but I didn't stay long to find out. I figured I ought to ride out and warn Phil here that there was likely to be big trouble. Those Maceys aren't here for reasons of their health. Foran's gettin' primed for a showdown and when he starts bringin' in top guns like this, he means to finish it.'

Frank scratched his chin pensively. 'I wonder how Frisco is goin' to take this. From what I know of the Maceys, they aren't likely to take to him bein' on the same payroll. They like to do things their way. They're both gunmen, not gunfighters.'

'Personally. I don't see any difference,' said Carson sourly.

Frank shrugged. 'There's a difference,' he affirmed. 'A gunfighter takes risks. They like to fight and kill for the sheer joy of it. But a gunman picks his time, makes sure his victim is nowhere near a gun when he strikes. His chore is just to kill, just that. He'll shoot a man in the back and think nothin' of it, just so long as he's in no danger to himself. Sure, the Maceys are fast with a gun, devil-fast. But they won't face up to a man in fair fight if they can do it another way.'

Fentry squinted up at him, his eyes bird-like in their curiosity. 'You aimin' to do anythin' about the Maceys, Condor?'

'Like what?'

'Like make sure they don't start any real trouble?'

Frank shook his head. 'This is none of my business,' he asserted. 'You've got a sheriff in town. I'm keepin' out of it.'

Fentry's eyes widened just a shade at that. There was a faint trace of sarcasm as he said thinly: 'Never figured I'd hear a marshal say that he'd stand by and let trouble start. Always thought once you were a lawman, you were always a lawman. Seems I must have been mistaken. You know damn well that Talbot doesn't stand a chance against men of their calibre.'

'Then maybe you should have picked yourself a better sheriff,' Frank retorted.

'I can see I'm just wasting my time,' snorted the old man. 'Except there may be one thing you ought to remember. If these gunmen should learn who you are, my guess is they'll come gunnin' for you – that is if Foran doesn't send them after you. Like you've just said, it won't matter much to them if you're carryin' a gun or not.'

'All this talk is goin' to get us nowhere,' Carson butted in sharply. He glanced at Frank. 'I'll get the cook to rustle you up food, Frank. Reckon you could do with a bite and a chance to bathe that scratched face of yours.'

Frank considered that for a moment, then shook his head. 'Thanks for the offer, Phil. But I figure I'd better be gettin' back into town. There's a little unfinished business I've got to take care of before nightfall.'

He turned on his heel, tipped his hat to the girl, then swung up easily into the saddle and gave his horse its head.

Fentry watched the cloud of white dust settle in Condor's wake, then turned to the rancher and said soberly, 'You know, I've got an idea, Phil, that there's something more on his mind than we know about. Something seems to have been troublin' him for a while now. I'd like to know what it is. Reckon I might feel easier in my mind if I did. It's not like a man such as that to change overnight into a *hombre* who couldn't care less what happens when there's no real law and order in town and a range war is on the point of busting out.'

By the time Frisco and the rest of the Double Circle crew had rounded up their spooked horses, the sun was well down and they drove their mounts furiously over the mesa, back to the ranch. Putting the horses into the corral, the men made their way across to the bunkhouse, while Frisco stepped into the house where Foran was waiting.

There was an angry scowl on the rancher's face as he saw that the other had returned empty-handed. His tone was like the lash of a whip as he asked: 'All right, Frisco. Where's the girl? I thought I asked you to make sure and bring her here, by force if necessary.'

'We ran into a spot of trouble,' declared the other sullenly. He touched his bandaged arm gingerly.

Foran's eyes took on a sneering expression. 'You took five men with you and you let a girl beat you. What sort of men did I hire?'

'It wasn't like that at all. Condor was there with the girl. He must've spotted us going after her. By the time we'd run her to earth, he was there with a rifle.'

'That's still no goddamn excuse. There were six of you against a man and a girl.'

'He had the drop on us when we rode in. Monet's dead and Flannaghan is badly hurt.'

'But you still let those two get away,' raged Foran. His eyes lit up with a sudden, savage anger. 'Now, I'll have to do things another way. If I had the girl here, I could have forced her old man to do anything. As it is, I'll have to wait until the Macey brothers get here. Then we'll ride out and put an end to Carson for good.'

'You signin' on the Maceys?' Frisco asked tautly. He locked his gaze with the other man's.

'That's the general idea. You got any objections to workin' with them?'

'Only that I don't like the way they operate,' Frisco answered thinly. He rolled himself a smoke with one hand, put a vesper to the cigarette and drew the smoke deep into his lungs, blowing it out in front of him. 'They've got a bad reputation. Seems to me that if there's anythin' that might force the other ranchers to band together against you, bringin' them in will do it.'

Foran shrugged disdainfully. 'Once I've got the Macey brothers working for me, the rest of the ranchers can do as they please. We'll wipe them all out without any trouble.'

'And this *hombre*, Condor?'

'He won't do anythin',' said the other positively. 'If he intended to make any play, he'd have done it by now. I still haven't been able to find out what happened to make him as he is, but it must have been somethin' pretty big to cause him to hang up his guns Like that. If he should step out of line, the Maceys will take care of that little chore for me.'

'Seems to me that once the Maceys get here, you won't be havin' any need for me and the rest of the boys.' The sullenness was back in the other's voice. 'They like to give the orders whenever they're hired to do a job.'

'They'll take their orders direct from me,' said Foran tightly. He looked down at the other's arm. 'You'd better get that wound cleaned up. And quit worryin' about the Macey brothers. I'll take care of them when they get here.'

'I hope so,' muttered Frisco. 'They could turn out to be more trouble than they're worth.' He left the room and from the window, Foran watched him drag his spurs across the courtyard as he made his way over to the pump.

The long, hot afternoon ran on as Frank Condor made his way back to town. By the time he climbed the low rise and came in sight of it, the sun was on the point of touching the blue-purple rims of the mountains and there was a cooling wind blowing into his face, easing the soreness where itching bites and sand had scoured at his grimy flesh. As he drew near to the town, he noticed at once, with a strange tingling along his nerves, the changed appearance of it. The place held a deserted, subdued look. The streets seemed empty except for a handful of horses tethered to the hitching rails outside the saloons and the solitary man who did show as Frank rode into the man-shy street gave a quick glance up and down the road before hurrying over to the other side, hesitating a moment on the boardwalk, then plunging into one of the buildings that fronted the street. Frank had the impression it had been Steadman, but at that distance he could not be sure.

A wary uneasiness prickled along his back and ruffled the small hairs on his neck. Instinctively, he tensed his shoulder muscles, then forced himself to relax. A shoulder was no shield against a slug, he tried to tell himself. As he drew level with the Fast Gun saloon, there came a sudden burst of raucous laughter from inside. The batwing doors were thrust open and a figure hurtled through them, landing on his face in the dust. One glance was enough to tell Frank that it was Sheriff Talbot. The lawman heaved himself painfully to his hands and knees, looked wildly about him for a moment, made as if to scuttle across the street in Frank's direction, then stopped instantly as the saloon doors opened again and a man appeared framed in the entrance. Again, the loud roar of laughter sounded and a harsh, grating voice called: 'Don't you go any place, Sheriff. We got a little unfinished business to attend to, right now.'

Frank recognized the man at once. Flint Macey. The gunman held a pistol in his right hand. Now he lowered the barrel until it was pointing directly at Talbot's head.

He grinned wolfishly. The sweat started out on the lawman's balding head and began to trickle down into his eyes. He made a futile effort to wipe it away, his lips moving but no sound coming out.

'You was sayin' somethin' in there about arrestin' us for murder,' snarled the other. 'Don't see you doin' anythin' about it now. What's wrong? Lost all your guts?' Shifting the gun a little, the other snapped, 'Get on your feet, lawman.'

Talbot hesitated for a moment, not sure of what was coming. Then he heaved himself on to his feet with an effort, swaying a little, his face scared. The gun in Macey's hand roared three times in quick succession, the bullets kicking up tiny spirts of dust around the sheriff's feet. Frantically, the other danced around to dodge the flying lead.

'That's it, Sheriff. Let everybody see you dance.' Behind Macey, his brother Clay stepped out on to the boardwalk to watch the fun.

'Why don't you pick on somebody your own size?' said Frank evenly. He crossed his arms on the saddle horn, stared down at the killer evenly.

It was a measure of their concentration in watching the sheriff's plight that neither of the killers had seen Frank sitting there in the saddle. Now Flint Macey lifted his head, glared up at the other. Then his eyes narrowed down. Lips thinned back, he snarled harshly, 'You say something, mister?'

'You know damn well I did,' Frank retorted. 'Seems to me you like nothin' better than pushin' around folk who're not in your class.'

'Meanin' you are?' The other stepped forward a couple of paces, ignoring the sheriff, who picked himself up and moved over to the far side of the street, dusting himself down with shaking fingers.

'Meanin' just that.'

Again, the other's lip curled sneeringly. 'Maybe you'd better step down here and try.'

From behind him, Clay Macey said sharply: 'He ain't wearin' any shootin' irons. Flint.' He peered up at Frank from beneath thick brows, drawn into a straight line of puzzlement. 'Seems to me I've seen this *hombre* someplace before. Can't place him though.'

'Makes no difference to me,' growled the other belligerently as Flank swung down from his mount. 'He's just horned in on trouble.'

'You usually shoot men who're unarmed?' Frank put naked scorn into his tone, aware that a small crowd had gathered on the boardwalk and other faces were peering from the windows overlooking the street. 'Reckon that's the only way you'll ever outdraw and outshoot a man, unless you were to let him have it in the back.' He was deliberately taunting the other, knew that the man facing him would pull the trigger without an instant's hesitation and with no more feeling than if he was shooting the head off a striking rattler.

Flint Macey let out a savage bull-like roar, then thrust the Colt back into leather. 'Then I think I'll just bust your head, fella,' he declared, leaping forward, big fists swinging.

Frank stepped inside the wildly flailing arms, delivering two sharp, jolting punches to the other man's face. The blows were short but they carried authority. Macey blinked, jerked to a standstill. His lips drew back over his teeth as blood spurted from his nose. There was a savage, dangerous look on his face now, a murderous hate in the deep-sunk eyes that stared piggishly at his adversary. Realizing that he would need cunning as well as his superior weight, he came in cautiously, hands held high, hoping to catch Frank in a bear hug and force him back on to the ground where he could use every dirty trick in the book.

Another hard blow hammered Macey's head back on his shoulders, but it did not lower his guard and before Frank could hit him again, a rock-like fist caught him on the side of the head, knocking him on one side. Shaking his head in an effort to clear it, he moved back, but not quickly enough. Macey hooked a foot behind his knee, swung him savagely off balance. Frank felt himself being hurled bodily towards the rails. His collision with them sent them crashing down and he hit the edge of the board-walk with the small of his back, all of Macey's two hundred and fifty pounds on top of him. The impact drove all of the wind from him. Instinctively, as he fell, he twisted over on to one side. his nose squashed against one of the wooden uprights. Fear spurred the numbness out of his limbs. With a tremendous effort, he managed to suck a little air down into his aching lungs, felt a stab of pain lance through his chest as he did so, knew that the fall had either bruised or cracked one of his ribs. There was the salt taste of blood in his mouth and as he spat it out a wave of saving anger seared through him, giving him the strength to lift one knee as the other attempted to kick him in the belly.

Macey's boot crashed on the side of his shin. Frank gasped in agony, felt his vision go dim, was only vaguely aware of the big figure standing hazily above him, preparing to kick him once more. Somehow, he succeeded in dredging up sufficient energy to roll over a couple of feet, landing hard up against the smashed rails. As his opponent thudded to the dirt with both knees bent under him, Frank grabbed at a flailing arm, hung on desperately with all of his remaining strength, sought to lever the other over his prone body. Macey howled loudly as the wrench on his arm almost pulled it from its socket. He reared up awkwardly, his face a mass of blood, giving him a ferocious appearance. Dimly, Frank was aware of Clay Macey yelling hoarsely, urging his brother on, but there was no time for him to take notice of this. Already, the killer had heaved himself up on to his knees, hauling himself up with his free hand. He tried to kick Frank in the groin; but still retaining his grip on the other's left arm, Frank twisted himself sharply, using his legs as leverage, jerking the man's arm tightly behind his back in a vicious hammer-lock. His vision cleared slowly as he held on grimly, knowing that once he released his hold, the advantage would rest with the other.

But even as he struggled to push himself to his feet, a boot stomped down on his outstretched hand where it rested on the boardwalk as Clay stepped in to aid his brother. Sucking in a gasp of pain, Frank was forced to let the big man go and Flint seized his chance, swung clear and stepped back, breathing heavily through his open mouth, eyes glinting. Only a few seconds elapsed before Macey renewed his attack, knowing that be still held the advantage.

Arms spread wide, he circled in, his gaze never once leaving Frank's face. Frank waited for him to come in, knowing that the other would use any dirty trick he could think up. This man had been marked by the scars of a score of battles such as this, knew all there was to know about in-fighting. Coming in, Macey feinted with his right hand, brought the left sweeping round. Frank ducked, saw the other's knee coming up as Macey rushed him, barely managed to twist aside as the thudding kneecap scraped along his thigh. Even as he staggered back, the other's outstretched arms clamped around his middle and thrusting his head well down under Frank's chin, the other began to exert pressure on his back, seeking to force him down. Frank felt his senses begin to swim, knew he would have to break that hold soon or perish. Grinning fiercely, Macey continued to squeeze, forcing Frank back towards the boardwalk.

Bracing himself, Frank got the heel of his right hand

under the other's jaw, thrust his head back with all of his remaining strength. Macey grimaced but held on, not yielding an inch. Curling his fingers, Frank gouged at the other's eyes, felt the slackening on the other's grasp. As the other's pressure eased, he brought his knee up sharply into the pit of the killer's stomach. Macey bleated, let go his hold, staggering back, his body bent forward as he strove to ease the agony in the mid-section. He was on the point of forcing himself to straighten up when Frank's bunched fist connected solidly with his exposed jaw. For a moment, the big man remained upright, swaying on his feet, his eyes glassy, his mouth gaping as he struggled to breathe through the fresh flow of blood that ran from his split lips. Then he toppled sideways and crashed full length in the dirt. From the way he fell, Frank knew he would not be conscious for some time. He turned away, conscious of the blood that oozed from his own battered face, thinking that the fight was over, but even as he turned to make his way from the scene, there was a soft movement behind him and before he could turn his head, the butt of a gun crashed against the back of his skull, pitching him forward on to his face.

Slowly, painfully slowly, consciousness returned and, as awareness flooded into his mind, the gnawing agony came with it. He tried to move, but the pain which lanced through his skull seemed to split it apart. Gasping, he opened his eyes and peered about him. He was lying on a low bed and there was someone at the other side of the room with his back to him. As the low groan emerged from his lips, the other turned and came forward. Through his blurred vision, he recognized Doc Fortune.

'Better lie still for a while, Frank. That was a nasty knock you took. If you hadn't got such a damn thick skull, we'd be gettin' you ready for Boot Hill right now.'

'What happened?' Gingerly, Frank put up a hand and touched the back of his head, wincing as the pain jarred again.

'You turned your back on Clay Macey. Lucky for you he didn't decide to put a slug in your back. He's a really slimy character.'

'You don't have to tell me that,' muttered Frank grimly. 'I know their kind of old.' With an effort, blinking rapidly, he forced himself into a sitting position. Gradually, the pain subsided into a dull, diffuse ache and he was able to see clearly. 'How long have I been out?'

'Best part of an hour,' declared the other. 'We brought you here after the Maceys had cleared town. From what I heard, they're ridin' out to join up with Foran.'

'You heard right. Judge Fentry was at Phil Carson's place when I left. He'd got word to him about these two polecats. He figured there might be trouble.'

'He figured right.' The other poured a glass of whisky, handed it to Frank, waited while he sipped it slowly. He did not go on until Frank had emptied the glass, then he took it from him, turned back to the table. He had something to tell him, but the telling of it was not going to be easy. A moment later, he turned, his face hard. 'There's somethin' you ought to know, Frank. The reason why those two killers had set about Talbot. He'd gone into the saloon to arrest 'em both for murder.'

'That was sure a fool thing to do,' Frank said sombrely. 'Talbot wasn't in their class when it comes to handlin' a gun. What made him do it?'

'They bushwhacked old Slim Edmond just after noon, shot him down without warning.'

'Slim – dead?' Frank sat wholly still as the other told him, his lips stretched thin and tight, his face a mask. He drew in a long breath, then turned his gaze away from Fortune and stared expressionlessly at the window. Only the white knuckles standing out in his hands gave any indication of the terrible depth of his feelings.

'You got any idea why they'd want to shoot him down, Doc?'

Fortune shook his head slowly. 'Far as I know, it was just a senseless killing with nothing behind it. I may be wrong, of course. Could be that Slim had fallen foul of those boys sometime in the past and this was a vengeance killing, but if he had, he never spoke of it to me.'

'Nor to me.' Frank's voice was icy cold. With an effort, he swung his legs to the floor, stood up, clinging for a moment to the bed for support as a wave of dizziness swept over him, accentuating the weariness in his battered and bruised body.

'What do you aim on doing, Frank?' There was a faint note of concern in the other's tone. He stepped forward to give him a helping hand but Condor waved it away with an impatient gesture.

'This is a chore I've got to finish,' he said tightly. 'Seems I've been livin' in a fools' paradise for the past year.'

3

The Avenging Gun

For a moment, after opening the drawer in his room, Frank stared down at the guns lying there, without reaching out to touch them. He had made a vow never to use them again after that shot which had killed his brother had been fired from them. Now it seemed that the fates which had been stalking him ever since had finally caught up with him. Almost savagely, he drew them out, buckled the heavy belt around his waist. Gently, he eased the weapons in the holsters, his hands moving almost of their own volition, swinging the guns clear of leather, thumbing back the hammers. The old skill was still there, never lost, not even after more than a year.

Opening the drawer a little wider, he found the star thrust at the back, drew it out, fingered it for a brief moment. Even though he'd thrown in that job back in Texas after the gunfight in which his brother had died, he still considered himself a lawman. At the back of his mind he figured that Talbot would raise no objections to having another gun on his side. Throwing back the flap of his jacket, he pinned the badge on to his shirt, let the jacket fall back into place, hiding the star.

He locked the door of his room after him, stepped out into the corridor, looking in both directions before making his way down the creaking stairs. The clerk, seated behind the desk, glanced at him curiously as he walked past, then went back to his perusal of the paper he had been reading. It was no business of his what the other did, but his eyes had widened just a shade as he noticed the heavy guns strapped to the other's waist. If there had been any sign that big trouble was due to hit Benton soon, that was surely it, he decided. He was vaguely glad that he was not the object of Condor's attentions.

Frank walked slowly in the direction of the square. He kept himself deliberately alert, for there was still the possibility that some of the Double Circle crew were around town and might pull off a dry-gulching as they had with Slim. He noticed the eyes of several of the townsfolk on him as he strode by, knew they were all wondering at the gunbelt low on his hip. Reaching the sheriff's office, he rapped on the door with his knuckles, then went inside. He caught Talbot in the act of rising hastily from behind his desk, his hand reaching for the gun on top of it. The other relaxed visibly when he saw who it was.

Without speaking, he sank down into his chair again, rubbing a hand over his chin. There was something about the man who stood in front of the desk which he had not seen before. But Talbot had been around long enough to be able to put his finger on this elusive quality. Frank Condor was completely co-ordinated. He was entirely confident – utterly deadly.

'I won't bother you with details, Sheriff,' Frank said even. 'I think you can guess why I'm here.'

'The Macey brothers.'

Frank nodded tersely. 'I want them on two counts, but only one matters at the moment. They bushwhacked my best friend in Benton.'

'I know.' Talbot sighed and leaned back resignedly. 'I

tried to bring 'em both in and you know what happened. I guess I'm gettin' a mite too old for this sort of business. But there's nobody else and—' He stopped. The other had leaned forward over the desk. his jacket falling open as he moved, and, for the first time, Talbot saw the star pinned on Frank's shirt. He gestured weakly towards the nearby chair.

'Sit down, Frank. I can see you've got somethin' else on your mind, otherwise you wouldn't be wearin' that badge. You're invitin' trouble with that around here. I suppose you know that.'

'I'm just beginnin' to realize a whole heap of things,' Frank said harshly. He fingered his bruised face tenderly. 'I know I don't have any authority in Benton. Matter of fact, I maybe don't have any authority anywhere now. But just so long as I'm wearin' this, I'm keepin' the right to gun down any man who gets in the way between me and the Maceys.'

'If it'll make you feel any better, I'll swear you in as my deputy. That way, it'll make things a little more legal. There are some of the Town Council who may baulk at the idea. One or two are almost certainly in Foran's pay. They didn't back down anyway when Blackie Carron and Frisco rode in and put on that fake trial with the two Carson boys.'

Frank shook his head. 'I'll stay as I am. There ain't no law I know of against gunnin' down killers. Seems like Foran is tryin' to make himself the law in this part of the territory anyway.' He paused, rolled a smoke, lit the cigarette and dragged the sweet-smelling smoke into his lungs. 'What about the other ranchers? Figure they would back me in this play?'

'Could be. You want me to talk to them, maybe get them into town where you can put the proposition to them yourself?'

Frank pondered that a moment, then got up. 'Do that,'

he said tightly. 'But don't waste time. Foran won't be standin' still now that he's got the Maceys on his payroll. My guess is he'll move against Phil Carson as soon as he figures he's got the edge on his side. Phil has plenty of men, but they're none of them gunfighters.'

'I'll see to it that as many of them as can are here tonight,' said the other enthusiastically. He stretched out a hand, gripped Frank's tightly. 'I'm real glad you've taken this step, Frank. You can rely on me to back up any play you make.'

Frank wasn't quite sure how much he could count on the other when things began to get really rough; but there was the fact that Talbot had gone into the saloon after those two killers when he had heard they had bush-whacked Slim, so there might be some courage left in the other yet. Trouble was, he was no longer as fast with a gun as he probably used to be and that could be a distinct disadvantage, not only as far as Talbot himself was concerned, but also for anyone who had to look out for the other when the lead started flying.

Leaving the office, he made his way to the store near the end of the street where he purchased some ammunition for the Colts, pressing the slugs into his belt until every loop was filled. This done, he made his way to the funeral parlour, to pay his lasts respects to the man he had come to know better than anyone else in Benton. The undertaker was a wizened little man with a permanent stoop. He always seemed to be wringing his hands together as though mutely apologising profusely for his calling.

'This is a bad business, Mister Condor,' he said in a high, nasal voice. 'A very bad business. I only wish I knew what it was all going to lead to. Believe me, before this is finished, there will be a lot more men lying there where he is now.'

Frank stared down in silence at Slim's face, now devoid

of all the marks of care and worry which it had borne in life. His brother had looked a little like that the last time he had seen him, he reminded himself. The ways of violence never changed, especially out here along the frontier. Men died and were buried, and then they were forgotten. The law of the jungle still prevailed, and for many men their lives depended on the speed of the hand and the accuracy of a tiny piece of lead, no bigger than the tip of his little finger.

He turned away from the coffin, sickened to his stomach at the utter senselessness and stupidity of it all. This, he told himself was the reason he had taken his guns and locked them away in the drawer in his room. Now the fates had taken another hand in the game and he had been forced by circumstances to take the guns out again, to make himself the target for a bullet from any direction. Thrusting his fingers into the gunbelt, he hitched it a little higher about his waist.

At the door of the undertaker's, he was accosted by a thinfaced man whom he recognized as one of the grooms at the livery stables.

'Frank Condor?' inquired the other breathlessly.

Frank nodded. 'That's right.'

'Sheriff Talbot asked me to find you. I was to tell you that Blackie Carron and some of the Double Circle boys are in town. He figures they may be lookin' for you.'

'You know where they are now?' Frank asked flatly. He let his gaze drift up and down the street.

'Carson's at Frenchy's right now. The rest of the boys were headed for the saloon last time I saw 'em.'

'Thanks.' Frank gave a brief nod. 'I'll take care of it.'

The other gave him a curious look as he stepped down into the street, but Frank had already forgotten him. There was the chance that he might be able to force Foran's hand. If he arrested Carron on a charge of lynching those two riders and locked him up in the town jail, it could throw all of Foran's well-laid plans out of gear, might even forestall any attack on Phil Carson's spread. Deliberately skirting the main street, he made his way around to the rear of Frenchy's place, a dingy rooming house that stood alone, separated from the buildings on either side, having been erected on a vacant plot when the town itself had been thrown up. Entering the rear door, he cat-footed to the stairs. paused as the owner, a tall, French-Canadian, came out of one of the back rooms. He opened his mouth in surprise as he caught sight of Frank, closed his mouth with a snap as one of the Colts leapt into the other's hand.

'I'm here on business, Frenchy,' he said tautly. 'So don't go tryin' to warn any of your customers.'

'You have no business here,' growled the other. He stared down unwinkingly into the barrel of the Colt.

'Then I'm makin' it my business as of now.' Frank flipped back his jacket to reveal the star. 'Now which room is Blackie Carron in?'

'He ain't here,' grunted out the other suddenly. He squared up to Frank.

'I happen to know he is.' Frank scarcely seemed to move, but the next moment his left hand had grabbed the other's shirt front, twisting it into a tight ball as he pulled the man closer to him, thrusting the barrel of the Colt against the loose skin at the base of his throat. His thumb tripped the hammer back with an ominous click. 'Guess you just made a mistake, Frenchy.'

He saw the other's adam's apple jerk as he swallowed convulsively. For the first time a look of fear appeared in his eyes. 'All right. So I made a mistake. He's upstairs. Second room on the left.'

'Alone?'

The other nodded wordlessly. Frank released his grip on him and the man staggered back against the wall, watching him out of hate-filled eyes. Frenchy got most of his custom from the Double Circle men, so it was only natural that he should side with them against him. Also, the shrewd French-Canadian had a good idea which side his bread was buttered, figured that whatever happened, Witney Foran was soon going to be the top man around Benton and he was not a man likely to forget his friends – or his enemies.

The smell of the place was musty and mildewed, with the remnant odours of a thousand things hanging in the still, unmoving air. Something scurried across the floor ahead of Frank as he reached the top of the stairs and stood quite still, listening around for any sign of movement. The door which Frenchy had indicated was closed and he tip-toed over to it, pressed his ear against it for a moment. There was no sound from inside. Was Blackie there or had he seen him coming and somehow guessed his intention? If the Double Circle ramrods were in town looking for him, it meant they had decided he was a menace that had to be got rid of as quickly as possible and it was unlikely they would relax their vigilance simply because he had, until a little while ago, gone around unarmed.

Then, as he stood there, he heard the creak of a bed spring. Gripping the door handle, Frank twisted it sharply, thrust the door open and stepped through, levelling the gun on the man who lay sprawled on the bed. Blackie started up as though shot, then sank back on to the bed, eyes smouldering.

'So somebody gave the little boy a gun,' he said sneeringly. 'I wondered when they'd get around to that. I suppose it was that fool Talbot who did this. Anythin' he's scared to do, he tries to pass on to somebody else.' He sucked on the cigarette he had been smoking. 'And now you've got the drop on me, what do you reckon you're goin' to do?'

'I figure the first thing will be to lock you up in the town jail. Then you'll answer to a charge of murder.'

The other grimaced. 'You've got no proof of that, Condor. You're bluffin' and I aim to call your bluff right now.' He made to swing his legs to the floor and get to his feet.

Frank thumbed the hammer back. 'I'm warnin' you, Carron. You make a move without my say-so and you'll stop lead. I've suddenly developed a palsied trigger-finger thinking over what you've been doin' around here and you can look on this badge here as a licence to kill.'

Carron stiffened abruptly. His hand which had been on the point of reaching out for the gunbelt hanging over the back of the nearby chair, halted in mid air. Stepping forward, Frank eased the twin Colts out of their holsters and tossed them into the corner of the room. 'Now get on to your feet. Make one move I don't like and I'll plug you.'

'You'll never get away with this and you know it, Condor. Put me in that jail and Witney Foran will be ridin' into town with so many men they'll put this place to the torch.' A murderous fury blazed up in the other's dark eyes, burned like a fire whipped up by the wind, then died as a crafty expression replaced it.

'Maybe he'll try,' Frank said evenly. He made a quick motion with the gun. 'Now move ahead of me, down the stairs and out into the street. Don't expect any help from Frenchy. I've already had a talk with that critter. He knows exactly what to expect if he tries anythin'. Reckon he's too fond of keeping his hide unperforated to bother about you right now.'

Some of the indolence left Carron. His mouth was firmly set as he moved slowly in the direction of the door with Frank's gun barrel poking him hard in the spine. At the door, he paused, half-turned. 'Why don't you get wise to yourself, Condor? You've got no call to like this town any more than we have. Just where do you fit into this affair?'

'Let's say I don't like snakes who make their livin'

shootin' men in the back like Slim Edmonds, or stringin' up badly wounded men whose only fault was that they weren't on Foran's side.'

'You're sure making one hell of a mistake doin' this,' Blackie grunted. 'You'll never get me to that jail. I've got men outside who'll drop you the minute you show your face outside the door of this place.'

'Maybe so. But there ain't a bullet made that could stop me from smashing your spine with one shot. So just ponder on that while you're goin' down the stairs.' He thrust the gun barrel a little harder into the foreman's back, felt the other wince, then move forward. Slowly, they made their way along the passage and down the stairs. Frenchy was nowhere to be seen as they went along the narrow hall towards the front door. For a moment, Frank wondered about the other. There was the possibility that he had slipped away to warn the other Double Circle men of what was happening. But he hadn't any time to think about that now. He had only to relax his vigilance for a moment and Carron would turn it to his advantage.

The street door was open and Carron went through slowly, Frank following close behind. In spite of his show of confidence, he was feeling somewhat uneasy in his mind. Carron was not the sort of man to go with him like this, without a fight. It seemed more probable that he knew his men had been warned and he was keeping his eyes open, ready to explode into action the moment somebody started shooting. It all added up to the possibility of there being half a dozen or so guns waiting out there for him among the lengthening shadows around the buildings on either side of the street and it reminded him of the sort of target his broad back made for any marksmen behind one of the windows or perched on the flat roofs.

'You still think you can go through with this, Condor?' sneered Carron. 'Seems to me that you're getting almighty nervous.'

'Then you'd better be careful it doesn't spread to my trigger finger,' retorted Frank. 'Walk along the boardwalk to the jail, Carron. Remember what I told you. The first sign of any trouble from those riders with you and you'll get the fast bullet.'

The length of street as far as the square was empty – ominously so – as the two men began to move slowly towards the jail. Frank ran his gaze slowly over the horses tied up outside the saloon. He recognized several of the Double Circle mounts but there was no sign of any of the crew. The shadows between the buildings lay thickly on the ground, plenty of places where men might lie in waiting. One of the horses at the hitch rail snorted suddenly, kicked out at the flies which buzzed in an irritating cloud about it. Almost as if the abrupt movement had been a signal, a voice yelled harshly:

'Condor!' The echoes chased themselves into silence among the houses.

Blackie Carron half turned his head. There was a grin on his fleshy features. 'Reckon you're in a spot now, Marshal,' he grated. 'Don't say I didn't warn you.'

'Just you keep on movin',' Frank said tightly. He had sighted the shadow thrown by this man just between the saloon and the grain store next door to it. 'Better warn those boys of yours that you get a bullet if they don't step out into the street with their hands lifted.'

'Go to hell,' snarled the big foreman savagely. He stood quite still in spite of the hard pressure of the gun barrel in his back.

'Step away from Blackie, Condor,' yelled the voice again. 'This is the last warnin' you're goin' to get. There are four guns trained on you.'

Frank hesitated for less than a second. He had just glimpsed another of the Double Circle men crouched on the roof of the livery stables a few yards further along the opposite side of the street. Before Carron could make a move, Frank reversed the gun in his hand, hitting Blackie on top of the skull with the butt, sending him sprawling to the slatted boardwalk. Even before the other's unconscious body had crashed to the ground, Frank was diving for the cover of the water trough a couple of feet away, skidding along the rough wood as bullets crashed over his head, embedding themselves in the slats. Something laid a burning touch along his upper arm. He flinched, but steadied himself long enough to loose off a shot at the man on the roof of the stables. He saw the other draw back sharply, drop his gun and clutch at an injured arm. Not good enough to put him out of action for good, Frank thought tautly. But it gave him enough time to divert his attention towards the man in the narrow alley. The gunhawk's pistol barked sharply and the slug whistled within an inch of Frank's head.

Leaving the unconscious foreman where he lay, he got his legs under him, thrust himself off the ground in one quick leap and ran for the narrow lane which adjoined the building, jumping away from splintering stone and whining lead as more bullets followed him. At the rear of the building, a sharply-angled wooden erection gave difficult access to the roof. Holstering the Colt, he jumped for the overhang, caught it with his fingers and hung there for a moment with every fibre of his arms screaming with the agony, then slowly succeeded in hauling himself up on to the overhanging bar, wriggling along it with his legs, steadying himself as he reached the far end. Now he was lying athwart the broad beam where it joined the wall less than four feet below the level of the roof. Even so, it was not going to be easy to make it.

Bracing himself, hanging on only by his legs, he eased himself up slowly, balancing like a wire-walker, then leapt into space, fingers clawing for the stone abutment which projected out from the corner of the roof. Clasping it, he hung there, sucking air into his lungs, then pulled himself up to safety with a wrenching of shoulder muscles. Bending low, he ran to the front of the building, crouched down near the stone parapet.

The man who had been hiding in the alley across the street was just visible now, a dark figure peering towards the rear of the building around which Frank had disappeared a few moments before. He was almost an open shot from that angle. Another two men were lying on their stomachs behind the horse trough further along the street and on the roof of the building almost directly opposite, he could make out the prone figure of the fourth gunman. If there were any other Double Circle riders around he could not see them.

Easing the Colt from its holster, he levelled it across his left arm, took quick aim at the man in the mouth of the alley and fired swiftly, saw the other suddenly arch as the bullet took him just above the heart. The gunhawk lifted slightly on splayed-out legs, planed backward under the leaden impact. He hit the dust with a sickening thud and lay still, his pistol jetting aimlessly at the sky. Frank had seen many men go down like that and not one of them had lived more than a few seconds afterwards.

But the shot had given away his position. The man on the opposite roof jerked up his gun, aimed and fired in the same fluid motion. The bullet ricocheted off the roof, the twisted slug of lead screaming over Frank's right shoulder. One of the men behind the horse trough yelled harshly, in a scared, high-pitched voice, jerking up his gun. Drawing himself into a half-crouch to expose as little as possible of his body to Frank's fire, he turned about and vanished into the saloon, the doors swinging shut behind him. His companion tried to do likewise, reached the slowly-swinging doors just as Frank's bullet took him in the back. He collapsed in an inert heap in the doorway, his gun falling from nerveless fingers.

Ignoring the splash of white-hot lead on the edge of the

parapet, Frank sighted on the man on the opposite roof. The other had thrust himself down behind one of the abutments with only part of his legs visible. Frank waited with ill-concealed impatience, the other Colt balanced in his hand now. There had been no time in which to reload the first. From where he lay, it was impossible to see what was going on in the street below. Most of the townsfolk who had been watching, had prudently vanished into the nearby buildings, scattering the instant gunplay started up. But Carron was still down there, unconscious it was true, but there was still a chance for one of his boys to sneak up directly beneath where Frank lay and take him away. He snapped a couple of shots at the gunhawk, aiming over an extended arm. The elevated brim of the other's hat disappeared, but it was impossible to tell whether or not he had been hit. It didn't seem likely. Scenting victory, Frank edged a little closer to the drop-off of the roof. Almost instantly, there was return fire from the man behind the opposite abutment. The man was evidently unhurt, but he was excited and began to fan.

Clenching his teeth in sudden frustration, Frank waited for the other to reappear, knowing he had the man pinned down, unable to move forward or backward without exposing himself. When the seconds had lengthened into a couple of minutes without any further move on the other's part, Frank decided there was only one way to force the man out into the open. Deliberately, he rose to his knees, his gaze fixed on the spot behind which the man lay.

'All right. Throw down your gun and lift your hands,' he yelled loudly.

The other's reaction was, as Frank had expected, immediate. He threw himself sideways as the man rose, lining up his gun on Frank. He was still in mid-air when he fired, saw the other stagger as he was hit, then tilt and sway drunkenly, pitching forward. For a split second he teetered on the very edge of the roof, then dropped forward into nothing. He hit the top of the boardwalk immediately beneath, crashed through it with a loud splintering of wood.

When there came no further movement from the street, he lowered himself from the roof on to the low veranda, then dropped lightly to the ground, moving over to the man on the far side of the street. As he neared the man he saw to his surprise that the other was not dead, although he was pretty near it. A faint groan escaped from the man's bloodless lips and he tried to roll over on to his back. His eyes were already glazing over, blood trickling from his mouth and dripping off his chin. His gun lay in the dust some feet away from his clawed fingers which groped blindly for it. There was something of deep hatred in the dark eyes as he paused, then fumbled beneath his jacket.

'Don't try it!' Frank warned. He knew the signs better than most. A small Derringer hidden in an arm holster.

The other did not seem to hear. With the last ounce of his strength, he struggled desperately, managed to half draw the small gun from its holster before the Colt in Frank's hand spoke again. The slug knocked the gunslinger back among the splintered wood, dead for sure this time.

Straightening up, Frank drew a deep breath into his lungs, pouched the smoking Colt. He turned to glance in the direction of the small group of men who had come tumbling through the doors of the saloon now that the gunfight was over, men who stared open-mouthed at the bodies in the street.

'Better fetch the undertaker,' Frank said thinly. He spun on his heel and walked back to where Blackie Carron still lay on his face. As he reached the foreman, the other pushed himself up on to his hands, his head hanging down between them. He shook himself feebly, lifted his head to stare up at the tall man standing over him.

'All right, Carron,' Frank snapped. 'On your feet. We've got an appointment with the sheriff.'

The other offered no reply. Sullenly, rubbing the back of his head, he staggered to his feet, stood swaying for a moment, staring about him at the scene of carnage in the street. There was a look of stunned surprise on his features as he moved along the street with Frank following close behind.

Not until Carron was safely locked in one of the cells at the rear of the sheriff's office, did Frank force himself to relax. Talbot replaced the bunch of keys on the book behind his desk. There was a troubled expression on his grizzled face.

'Somehow, I'm not sure whether this was a wise move on your part or not, Frank. Witney Foran is sure goin' to be as mad as hell when he hears about this little episode. He won't rest until he's got Carron out of jail and fixed you for killin' his boys.'

'That's the way I'm figurin' it too,' Frank affirmed. 'It may serve to force his hand. And when a man's made to act without thinkin', out of pure rage, he's liable to make mistakes. That's what I'll be waitin' for.'

'Just so long as you know what you're doin',' grunted the other. 'You say one of 'em managed to get away. You can bank on Foran knowin' about this before nightfall. Hope you weren't plannin' on leavin' town for a while. If you were to leave us at the mercy of the Double Circle crew, this town wouldn't be in one piece by mornin'.'

'You've no need to worry on that score. I don't aim to leave until I know what Foran is aimin' to do.'

'Good.' The other was plainly relieved at this. 'I've got some of the ranchers comin' into town shortly after dark. Reckon they don't want to be seen abroad until they hear your proposition. Can't say I blame 'em. This Foran is a tough man to cross. I'd sooner step on the tail of a rattler than go up against him; and most of these men feel the same way. They've seen what he can do to get what he wants. Reckon a lot of the smaller men figure that they're too unimportant for him to worry about, that he won't want to grab off their bit of land and water if he can get his hands on Carson's place. Maybe you can get them to change their minds, but you won't find it easy.'

'They've got to know the score sooner or later. No use stickin' their heads in the sand and thinkin' there's no danger just because they're small fry. If they do that, he'll simply pick 'em off one at a time without any trouble. Now he's got the Macey brothers to back his play, as well as Frisco, he'll be feelin' pretty confident of himself.'

Frank Condor made his way slowly to the livery stables. It was almost dark now. The sun had vanished in a blaze of reds and scarlets to the west half an hour earlier and now night was rushing in from the north and east to swamp all of the glowing colours, leaving first the deepening purple and then the black with the first sky sentinels beginning to show directly overhead. Around him, the town was quiet. Too quiet. It spoke loudly of hidden menace and danger, of dark, deep shadows where men might hide, waiting to put a slug into his back without any warning. But he walked with a firm tread and tried not to show any of the tight uneasiness in his mind. He did not underestimate Foran. To have done that would have proved fatal. The other was no fool and he would never have got to be where he was by taking any unnecessary chances.

There was a riotous tumult of thoughts and ideas racing through his mind as he walked the quiet street of Benton. Had Foran learned of what had happened in town that afternoon? Even if he had, would he consider Carron's freedom more important in his scheme of things than riding against Phil Carson? There was the chance that he had gathered his men together and was even then on his way into town, determined to destroy the place and break his foreman out of jail. Inwardly, Frank was hoping that he would do none of these things. Knowing the way in which Foran's mind worked, there was just a slim chance he would decide that until Frank Condor was out of the way for good, he might always be on the defensive and that would not sit well with a man of Foran's calibre. If this was indeed the case, then his first chore would be to come looking for him. With him out of the way, his road would be clear.

Stepping into the dark, warm shadows of the stables, he leaned against one of the tall wooden uprights and built himself a smoke, rolling the cigarette several times between his fingers before licking the paper and thrusting it between his lips. He did not feel like smoking at the moment, but a cigarette could have its uses.

A dark shape drifted from the rear of the stables and a moment later, the groom stood beside him, eyeing him curiously.

'Thought I recognized you, Marshal,' muttered the other softly. He looked apprehensively up and down the deserted street. 'You expectin' trouble?'

'I always expect trouble when a place is as quiet as this.' Reaching into his pocket for a vesper, Frank struck it and touched the flame to the end of the cigarette. He flipped the spent match away. 'It's more'n likely that Foran will ride into town with some of his boys. I'm hopin' to be ready for him when he does.'

The other looked startled. 'You must be mad to take on that bunch alone.' His eyes narrowed on Frank in sudden appraisal, and opened wider. 'I saw what happened this afternoon. Pretty fancy shootin', by Godfrey, Marshal. But you'll need more'n that to take on this bunch of hard-cases. You heard that Flint and Clay Macey have joined up with him?'

'I heard,' Frank said tonelessly. 'I got an old score to settle with that pair when we meet up again.'

The other gave a brief nod of his head. He held his silence for a matter of minutes, and at last said: 'Guess this is as good a place to keep an eye on the street as any.'

'So I figured.' He made to say something more, then reached out and clamped a tight hold on the groom's arm, urging him to remain silent. There was the faint sound of riders in the distance, approaching at a fast pace.

Squinting into the encroaching darkness, he waited tensely. A few moments later, he saw the dust cloud thrown up by the oncoming horses. There were, he reckoned, a dozen men or so in the tightly-knit bunch.

'That's Foran all right,' whispered the man beside him. He eased his way back into the darkness of the stables as Frank released his grip. A few seconds later, he was gone. Frank grinned faintly to himself as he dropped the cigarette and ground it out under his heel, crushing it into the dirt. His fingertips brushed the butts of the Colts at his waist. The men rode along the main street without slackening their pace, their faces touched alternately by light and shadow as they passed before the many lamplit windows. As they drew level, Frank recognized the tall, expensively-dressed figure of Witney Foran in the lead. The other reined up his mount sharply before the sheriff's office, but did not get down. Instead, he sat straight in the saddle, motioned to the rest of the men with him to spread out a little, then called in a loud, ringing voice:

'Step outside, Condor. I want a word with you.'

Remaining in the dark shadows, Frank eased both guns from their holsters, called softly: 'I'm right behind you, Foran. Don't make any sudden moves and you won't get a bullet in the back. That goes for the men with you.'

He saw the other stiffen suddenly in the saddle, remain taut, not turning his head. Eventually, Foran said: 'You can't down every one of us, Condor, no matter how good you, are.'

'Maybe not. But I can sure plant a bullet in your back

before any of your men can get me. Now state your business and then ride on out of town.'

A pause, full of meaning. then the other said harshly: 'I've come for my foreman, Condor. I don't intend to leave without him. Fetch him out of jail and there'll be no trouble. Refuse, and I'll turn my boys loose. If I do that, you won't have much of a town left by morning, I can promise you.'

'Sorry. Carron stays where he is until his trial.'

'You've got no right to hold him and you know it. Talbot's the law in this town, not a jumped-up marshal who ain't even got the authority to wear a badge. You lost that right when you ran out on your job back in Texas. I've been checkin' up on you, Condor. I know everythin' there is to know about you. You're just a yeller-livered lawman who turned and ran when the goin' got rough.'

'If that's what you think, then just make one funny move and find out for yourself.'

'You're bluffin'.' There was a faint edge of uncertainty in the rancher's tone now which was not lost on Frank. 'For one thing. I know how you men work. You want to prove you're a fast gun, so you wouldn't shoot a man in the back, a man without a gun in his hand. That would sure spoil any reputation you've got. Besides, one man doesn't have a chance against eleven.'

'Two men, Foran,' called another voice, coming from Frank's right. A moment passed before he recognized it as belonging to Sheriff Talbot. Somehow, the other must have left the office and sneaked away around to the alley. Now he appeared in the faint light of the street. There was a shotgun in his hands levelled directly at the bunch in front of the building. 'This here scattergun will make one hell of a mess of most of you if I was to pull the triggers. Now just do like the marshal says, boys, turn your mounts and hightail it out of town before I get a mite too nervous.'

Slowly, Frank stepped up behind the mounted men. A

little of the tension drained out of him as he watched the Double Circle men wilt a little in the face of that terrible weapon in the sheriff's hands. A Colt or a rifle they were quite prepared to face, but not the destruction caused by one of those guns. At that close range, Talbot was unlikely to miss.

Foran stared down at the sheriff, venom in his glance. Through tightly-clenched teeth, he snarled, 'You'll regret this to your dyin' day, Talbot. I figured you to have more sense than to try to go up against me. Seems I was wrong.'

'Guess you've been wrong about a heap of things, Foran,' retorted the other sharply. 'You and your hired killers have been ridin' roughshod over us for long enough. Now it's our turn. Set one foot in Benton again, and I'm liable to blow your head off.'

'That's real fine talk.' Flint Macey leaned forward over his pommel, addressing himself to Talbot. 'Reckon I should've finished the job that I started this afternoon. But just remember this. We all make mistakes, sooner or later, and one of these days, I'll meet up with you again, when you don't have a shotgun in your hands and without Condor to back you up. Then you and me will have this out.'

There was a faint sheen of perspiration on the sheriff's face at the other's words. but he held his ground defiantly. The shotgun never wavered.

'Get movin',' he ordered tensely. 'I'll count up to ten. Any one of you still here by then will get a face full of lead.'

Foran tightened his lips, then abruptly dragged on the reins, jerking his mount's head around cruelly. 'All right, boys,' he said thinly. 'We now know where we stand with this hombre. I won't forget this. Talbot. Maybe you don't know it right now, but you've just signed your death warrant.'

Kicking spurs to his horse's flanks, he drove it along the dusty street, the rest of his crew following him. Frank watched as they thundered out of town, then thrust the guns back into leather. He turned to the other as Talbot lowered the shotgun reluctantly. Grinning faintly, he said: 'You put on a pretty good show there, old-timer. But we forced him to stand down.'

Talbot nodded his head a trifle shakily. 'Weren't nothin' else I could do and still live with myself,' he muttered simply. Turning, he stepped into the office with Frank at his heels.

After putting the gun back in the rack, he sank weakly into his chair, poured himself a glass of whiskey and downed it at a single gulp. grimacing as the raw liquor hit the back of his throat. 'I needed that,' he said hoarsely. 'Care for one yourself?'

Frank nodded, lowering his long body into the other chair, studying the other in the light of the oil lamp. He could guess at the effort it must have cost Talbot to do what he had just done. It was one thing to go against Foran, but another to brace him in the presence of the rest of his hired gunslingers.

Finally, the sheriff stirred himself. His hand shook a little as he poured a second glass, but he forced himself to steady it. 'Some of the ranchers rode in half an hour ago, Frank. They're at the hotel right now. You want to talk to them right away?'

'The sooner the better. I always reckon it's best to strike while the iron is hot. We've shown Foran that we mean business, but that won't stop him for long. Once the townsfolk see that he can't have things all his own way they're liable to get around to thinkin' that maybe he can be licked, after all. That's the one thing he's afraid of right now.'

'I guess you're right.' Talbot watched the other grow cold, keen. There was something really deadly about Frank Condor now, he decided. He had already made up his mind that if there was one man who might have a chance to save Benton and the surrounding territory, this was him. He glanced at the half-empty whiskey bottle for a lingering moment, then as if he had fought a mental battle within himself, he shook his head, picked it up and put it away in the cupboard behind him. 'I'll take you along to them.'

Cupping his hand around the top of the lamp, he blew it out. There was just enough light filtering on to the floor through the windows for them to see by as they made their way to the door and out into the street.

4
Stampede!

There were six men gathered in one of the upper rooms of the hotel when Frank Condor pushed open the door and stepped inside, with the portly sheriff close on his heels. Cigar and cigarette smoke curled thickly in the air, shining bluely in the light of the two lamps set on the low table. There were stout wooden shutters across the windows so that not a chink of light showed through. Frank noticed this precaution with a feeling of relief. It was evident that these men were not prone to taking unnecessary chances, especially where their own liveli-hoods were at stake, yet there was something on each of their faces which told him clearly that they were men who had come out to this stretch of territory when it was noth-ing more than raw, untamed wilderness, and they had taken it and beaten it into shape by sheer guts and hard work.

Now there was danger looming over it all, with the added threat of losing all they had fought and worked so hard for. If only he could put forward a sufficiently convincing argument, he might yet swing them all on to his side; or at least most of them.

Frank knew some of them by name, nodded a greeting as he sat down. He glanced across at Talbot. The sheriff

83

cleared his throat noisily, then said: 'I guess we all know why we're here. Frank has a proposition to put to you. It concerns Witney Foran.'

'We guessed as much as that.' Regan, short and balding, gave Frank a hard-bright stare. his gimlet eyes boring into the marshal. 'We also know the sort of man Foran is. A cold-blooded killer like those other men on his payroll. Still, I reckon we ought to let you speak your piece, Marshal. Nothin' to lose by just listenin'.'

'I'm hopin' that by the time you've all heard me out, you'll do more than listen,' Frank said quietly. 'As I see it, this could be a matter of life and death as far as you are concerned, both collectively as well as individually. Foran is gettin' all set to take over this territory. He's been bringin' in men from as far south as the Mexico border to back him up. He's got everythin' to gain and virtually nothin' to lose by startin' a range war here in Benton and running you all off your land.'

'What makes you think he's interested in us?' asked Credin, leaning forward in his chair, his face serious. 'He's made no move in my direction that I know of and my land is out near the edge of the Badlands, scarcely any use to a man as big as he is.'

'That's where you're wrong, where you could all be makin' the biggest mistake of your lives. Foran won't stop at pickin' off the best land. He wants to be the undisputed boss of everything. When he's got all of the land. he'll take over the town. You don't stop a man like that by hoping he'll take no notice of you. There's only one way to beat him and that's for you all to band together, fight him.'

'You sure talk big for a man who's only just started packing a gun around town,' said Credin. He looked and sounded unconvinced by the other's argument. 'I don't aim to get all of my men, and myself, killed. It would be sheer suicide to go against him with all of those hired killers at his back.' He stared at the redly glowing tip of his cigar.

Stone, seated near the wall said: 'I'm inclined to agree with Credin. We don't stand a snowball in hell's chance.'

Frank sighed. As Talbot had said, it was going to be harder than he had thought to convince these men. Maybe if he had been in their shoes, he would have thought the same way. They were small men, content to graze their herds on small spreads, wanting nothing more than to be left in peace. So far, Foran had played it clever, moved in against only a few ranchers, ignoring the others. There was no incentive for these men to risk everything by fighting what must seem to them a suicidal battle against insuperable odds. Yet somehow he had to make them see the light.

'I'll agree that it looks that way on the surface,' he admitted slowly. 'But you've got to see this thing in its proper perspective. Foran's being clever. He's lettin' you think you're safe so long as you leave him alone. But all the time you're doin' that, he's getting bigger and stronger every day with more men ridin' in. But he isn't God, you know. He lost three men today and Blackie Carron is locked away in jail. waiting to stand his trial for murder.'

'You've got Foran's foreman in jail?' There was a faint note of incredulous disbelief in Credin's voice. He looked startled. Swinging his gaze on Talbot, he went on: 'How long do you reckon you can hold him there once Foran gets to hear about it?'

'Foran already knows,' Frank said incisively. 'He rode into town a little while ago to try to bust Blackie out. He left in rather a hurry with his tail tucked between his legs.' He saw the men exchange glances full of meaning.

'Is that right, Sheriff?' asked Regan.

Talbot nodded 'It's right enough. Judge Fentry is out at Phil Carson's place right now. Once he gets back into town, Carron will stand trial. If he's found guilty – and this time it's goin' to be a real legal trial – then we'll hang him.'

'Reckon this puts a different light on the matter.' Regan nodded, his eyes pinched a little, hiding the thoughts behind them. Twin lines creased his forehead. 'I'll admit I've been worried about Foran for some time. His spread borders mine along the banks of the Red. If what you say is true, Condor, then we shall have to fight to protect what we have.'

'I'm not so sure.' Stone got to his feet, took a couple of nervous turns around the room, puffing hard on his cigar. 'Like you said a few moments ago, Marshal, Foran's got nothin' to lose by fighting. We've got everything. Seems a lot to put at stake on the slim chance that we might come out on top if we start anything. I've got a dozen men behind me, but none of them are gunmen like those Foran has.'

'Don't you see?' Frank said harshly. 'That's why you have to act together. Individually, you'd go down. Foran has perhaps forty men at his back. If you act together, you'll have almost three times that number.'

'Even so somebody is sure to get killed. I've known range wars before and what came after.'

Frank showed him a quick, straight glance. 'I know how you feel. There's plenty of it that I don't like. But believe me, there is no other way of doing it. Foran is all cocked for violence and nothing is going to stop that. All we can do is try to be ready to meet it when it does come.'

There was silence in the room for several minutes after that. Frank tried to read something into their faces, but they were inscrutable. Finally, it was Credin who spoke. 'I'm sure we've all taken to heart what you've said, Marshal. And I'll admit that most of it makes sense of a sort. Speaking for myself, I'm not so sure your idea is a good one. When it comes to going up against seasoned killers like the Maceys and Frisco, I'd like to be certain that the odds are tipped a little more in our favour than they seem to be at present.'

'So what are you trying to say?' Frank asked, his tone hard.

'Just this. You've got Blackie Carron in jail awaiting trial. Ain't no doubt in my mind that you could make that charge stick. Just the same, I don't doubt that Foran won't let you hang him, even if you was to find him guilty. So you go through with this, give Carron what he deserves and when I see him hanged, I'll back you to the hilt.'

He turned his head as he spoke, looked from one man to the other. Without exception, they nodded their heads in approval.

Frank shrugged his shoulders. In a way, he hadn't expected this much.

'Very well, if that's the way you want it,' he agreed reluctantly. 'I don't suppose there's any more to be said.' He rose to his feet.

As he reached the door, Credin stepped up to him. 'No hard feelings, Marshal. But I've spent almost a whole lifetime building up that spread of mine. It isn't much, but it's all I've got in the world. I don't want to risk throwing it away on a hunch, no matter how good you might make it sound.'

Outside, in the dark street, Frank stood for a moment while Talbot came out to join him. It was difficult to suppress the sense of disappointment he felt. As the other fell into step beside him, Talbot said: 'Don't take it too badly, Frank. They're frightened. They're up against somethin' so big, that they don't know what to do for the best. You can't really blame any of 'em. Foran is a big man around here and he'll turn his hired killers loose at the slightest provocation.'

'I'm not blamin' them for that; only for bein' so goddamn short-sighted that they can't see where their folly is leading them,' Frank retorted. 'This is something these men have got to face up to if they want to go on living peaceful and decent lives. Folks have got to sacrifice and they've got to take risks.'

Talbot turned his head and gave Frank a shrewd glance. When he spoke, his tone was soft and serious. 'Have you ever stopped to ask yourself why you're so keen to fight Foran and his men, Frank? If you have, then you'll know that for you it's revenge. Nothing else. I'm not so sure that you're really worried about this town. It's not done much for you all the time you've been in it. But when Slim was shot down without a chance, you suddenly took it on yourself to fight Foran and everything that he stands for. Vengeance' – he went on sagely – 'can be a pretty potent force. Much more so than the chance, which these fellas see as pretty remote at the moment, of having their ranches taken away from them by force.'

'I get the picture,' Frank said brusquely. He looked along the street to where a light shone in the small window of the diner. 'Let's get ourselves a bite to eat. I'm starved.'

Dawn was still only a faint grey smudge along the serrated eastern horizon the following morning when Frank Condor drifted his mount from the livery stables and headed out of Benton. Since leaving Talbot shortly before one o'clock that morning, the rest of the night had been quiet and uneventful. Foran seemed to have ridden back to the Double Circle spread, nursing his rage. In spite of the quietness, Frank felt some misgivings. The possibility that Foran might turn savagely like a cornered rattler and strike in blind fury at Phil Carson was not far from his mind and since he also wanted Judge Fentry back in town so that Carron's trial might take place as soon as possible had prompted him to forego any sleep and ride out to Carson's place.

The fact that he had not slept for more than twenty-four hours had little effect on him, beyond a dull tightness behind his eyes. In his time, there had been many occasions when he had trailed a man from one end of Texas to the other, when he had dozed in the saddle, covering long distances each day. Now this experience was standing him in good stead.

Two miles out of town, he was among the low, hump-backed ridges which lay athwart the start of the Badlands. The flat beds of the claypans were heaved and cracked from the long drought and in every direction the tufted grama grass was burnt and withered, curling and shrivelling to a dull coppery hue which came of long periods without moisture. His mount picked its way carefully along the well-stamped trail that wound in and out of the jagged clefts and half an hour later, with the swollen red disc of the sun just lifting above the saw-toothed crests of the hills. he came out of the ridges and found himself poised on the edge of the wide valley that lay in a huge, saucer-shaped depression before him. Yellow sand hills rose around the vast perimeter, running across the trail like waves in some gigantic ocean, the entire surface of the valley dotted with slowly drifting clouds of dust as wind eddies caught them and whirled them from one side to the other. He paused for a moment, easing himself up in the saddle, feet locked straight in the stirrups, letting his gaze move from one side to the other, eyes taking in every detail. The horse stood hipshot, resting after the hard journey over the inhospitable terrain.

For a moment, it seemed that nothing moved in the bluehazed distance. Then his keen eyes caught the faintest flicker of movement, not on the ground where he had been expecting it, but in the faintly-shimmering air where a small flock of zopilote buzzards wheeled and hovered on silent wings, dipping and rising again, circling over a dark speck perhaps two miles distant. Gently kicking the mount, he heeled it forward down the slope in a quick trot, peering anxiously ahead. There was no mistaking the meaning behind those clustering buzzards. From past experience, Frank knew only too well what their presence spelled out.

The birds rose swiftly at his coming, circled off a little distance away, still watchful, hovering on almost still wings in a wide mass. Now Frank could make out the twisted bundle of human flesh that lay, almost completely wedged in a small hollow, arms thrust out straight, fingers clawed into the sand in a last spasm of death agony. Sliding from the saddle, Frank approached the other slowly, bent over the dead man and turned him over gently. He felt the shock of surprise travel swiftly through him as he recognized Judge Fentry. The man had been shot in the chest from extremely close range. There were powder burns on the front of his shirt around the red-soaked edges of the tattered cloth.

Squatting there angrily beside the dead man, Frank tried to figure out what must have happened. The small gun which the other always carried beneath his left arm was still in its holster. He took it out and examined it closely, saw that it had not been fired. Fentry clearly had never had a chance to defend himself. Yet whoever had done this deed must have got within a few feet of him when the judge had been shot down. Straightening, Frank cast an experienced eye over the surrounding terrain. The prints of the judge's mount were clearly discernible leading back to the west, over towards the lip of the basin some three miles away, and off to his right, deeper tracks which told of a swiftly running horse. Evidently the tracks of Fentry's horse after he had been shot down. Moving over to the low rocks a few yards away, he clambered cautiously among them and on the far side found what he was looking for. Here the tracks were confused; at least two horses had been tethered there, he could see the marks where ropes had trailed across the sand and there were also boot-marks leading up to the hard rocks.

It looked like an ambush, yet there were some disturbing features about the set-up. Even from the top of the rocks, a shot would leave no powder burns on a man's shirt. The killer must have got a lot closer than that, which meant he had approached within clear sight of the judge when he had loosed off that fatal shot. All of which pointed to one of two possibilities. Either the killer had been someone Fentry knew intimately and had not suspected, or the second man had been holding a gun on him when he had been shot by his accomplice.

Pursing his lips into a thin, hard line, he went back to the body, lifted it across his saddle and remounted. There were questions which needed answering; important, urgent questions. He gave the horse its head, rode swiftly across the broad valley, up through the pine and manzanita on the far edge and down the slopes to the Carson spread, hauling up the bay in the courtyard. A few seconds later, the door of the ranch house opened and Phil Carson came out with Atalanta close behind him. Stepping down, Frank walked over to them.

'It's Judge Fentry,' he said tonelessly, jerking a thumb behind him. 'I found him among the claypans.' He saw the look of stunned shock on Phil's face, heard the girl's sharp intake of horrified breath. As she stepped down off the porch and made to go towards the horse, he said quickly: 'I wouldn't go any further, Atalanta. It ain't a nice sight.' Glancing back to the tall rancher, he went on: 'He was shot from real close range. Powder burns on his shirt. Guess he never had a chance.'

'You any idea who might have done this?' inquired Carson.

Frank shrugged expressively. 'Any one of Foran's men. Maybe even Foran himself.' Briefly, he related what had happened when Foran had ridden into town to try to get Carron out of jail, ending with: 'So you can see that he wanted Fentry out of the way pretty badly. Once we got around to tryin' Carron for the murder of your two boys, he'd be really up against it. The other ranchers have agreed to come in with us if we hang Carron for murder.'

'And without Judge Fentry to preside over the court, you can't do that until we get a circuit judge to come around into Benton and that could take weeks,' Atalanta said, nodding.

'Exactly. Somehow, he found out that Fentry was here overnight and they bushwhacked him as he was on his way back into town.'

'Once the others hear of this, they'll crawfish out of their deal,' Phil said pointedly. 'You can bet your last dollar on that. Foran's reasserted himself as boss around here and they'll run like scared rabbits.'

'That's so.' Frank nodded emotionlessly. 'On the other hand, nobody in town knows that the judge has been shot. That's the reason I brought him here instead of takin' him back with me.'

'Just what have you got in mind?' Carson looked puzzled. 'Fentry's dead. Nothing's goin' to alter that fact.'

'No. But if we was to bury him here, nobody would be any the wiser until the job of breakin' Foran is done. Foran can't spread it around that he's been killed without implicatin' himself in his murder. It won't be easy. There'll be a heap of talk in town when he doesn't show up, but if we can play our cards right we might be able to hold 'em off long enough to get the other ranchers to back us.'

Carson rubbed his chin thoughtfully. There was a speculative look in his deep-set eyes. Finally, he nodded in reluctant agreement. 'Reckon we've got no other choice in the matter,' he said at length. 'I'll get a couple of the boys to bury him. What do you intend to do in the meantime?'

'Guess I'd better head back for town as soon as you've given me a few answers to one or two questions.'

'I'll get you something to eat,' Atalanta said quietly. She seemed to have composed herself now. Going back into the house, she closed the door behind her. Frank could hear her a few moments later in the kitchen.

Carson indicated the seat on the porch. 'Sit down, Frank,' he said thinly. The lines on his forehead and around the corners of his mouth had grown deeper and the look on his face was not a pleasant one. 'Things are sure comin' to a head,' he said solemnly. 'I never figured anythin' like this would happen.'

'What time did Fentry leave here, Phil?' Frank lit a cigarette, dragged hard on it as he stared off into the glaring sunlight which lay in a vast yellow wave over the courtyard.

'Shortly after first light. He was in a hurry to get back into town. He had a feeling that there was more big trouble brewin'. But we neither of us thought it would be anythin' like this.'

Frank nodded musingly. 'That means he couldn't have been dead long before I came across his body.'

'Sure looks that way,' agreed the other. He stared fixedly ahead of him.

With the cigarette burning between his lips, Frank inhaled time after time, the smoke-laden breaths becoming deeper and deeper as he pondered on the problem, until his eyes began to water and his head swim. He knew he was unconsciously punishing himself for his gross stupidity. If only he had had his wits about him, he might have foreseen that Fentry would have been the object of Foran's next killing. The judge had clearly been the key figure in the coming drama. Now that he was dead, their problems had increased a hundredfold. He could see the difficulties which stretched ahead of him, wondered what he had let himself in for when he had taken those guns out of the drawer and pinned on the star once more. Perhaps he ought to forget this job, his scruples – even the oath he had taken to uphold the law so long ago – and ride on out of this place. The trouble was, a man could only run so far and then he had to stop, take stock of himself, look deep within his heart and ask himself whether he liked what he saw there.

He was still wondering vaguely whether there was a possibility of escape from his responsibility and conscience when Atalanta called from the kitchen. Getting heavily, wearily, to his feet, he followed Carson inside, throwing the butt of his smoke away.

Breakfast was eaten in the small dining-room next to the kitchen. But in spite of the appetising smell of the food and his own hunger, he ate without relish. When he had finished, he scraped back his chair and rose to his feet.

'That was a mighty fine meal, Atalanta,' he said, smiling. 'Made me realize just how hungry I was.'

She looked at him for a long moment, then said: 'You know you should do that more often, Frank.'

'Do what?' he asked, puzzled.

'Smile. It changes your whole appearance, makes you seem more—' She broke off in sudden embarrassment. 'Oh, I don't know: More human, maybe. More approachable.'

'Guess I haven't had much to smile about for some time now, Atalanta,' he told her seriously. 'Reckon there won't be much time either until this show is over, one way or the other.'

'You really think that Foran intends to fight and wipe us all out simply because we won't give in to him?'

'I'm afraid so. That's the sort of man he is. A man's life means nothin' to him if it stands in the way of him gettin' all he wants. Nor a woman's life either. He's got the habits of a prairie wolf. He kills just for the sake of killing. Maybe he hasn't shot all that many men personally, but the way I figure it, the man who gives the orders to his hired guns is just as guilty of murder as if he had pulled the trigger himself.'

He saw the troubled look on the girl's face as she accompanied him to the door and out on to the porch. 'Don't worry,' he said gently. 'I reckon that with a little luck, we'll stop him before this flares up into a full-scale range war and too many people get hurt.'

'Perhaps it's wrong of me to say this, but I'm more worried about you than of what might happen to me,' she said simply.

He turned slowly at her words, saw that she was looking at him with a curious shine in her eyes. Acting on impulse, he moved closer to her, put his hands gently on her shoulders, bent and kissed her full on the lips. She made no attempt to move away from him, rather she clung to him tightly and there was a response to her lips as Frank's mouth clung to hers for a long moment. Finally letting her go, he held her at arm's length, looked down into her face.

'Be careful, Frank,' she whispered softly. 'Very careful. Except for my father, you're only one man against the whole might of Foran's gunmen. They won't stop until they've killed you.'

'They won't find it easy,' he promised her. He turned his head and threw a swift glance at the sun, lighting the distant hills and already beginning to climb up to its burning zenith. 'I'll have to be ridin' now. I want you to promise me you'll stay here until this is all over. You saw what happened to Judge Fentry. Foran's killers won't stop just because it's a woman.'

'I'm not afraid of them,' she said quietly. She stepped forward, resting her hands on the low rail. 'This is such a beautiful country. It seems wrong that a man like Foran can ride in and bring such trouble.'

'There'll come a time when men like him are gone and forgotten,' Frank said soberly. 'But whenever men move into a new country like this, they always have to fight to keep it clean and decent. The vultures always move in first.'

He stepped down into the courtyard to where his mount was waiting. From somewhere out of sight, on the

slope of the low hill behind the barn, there came the
sound of shovels biting into the soft earth. Carson's men
were hard at work digging a grave for Fentry. For a
moment, his nails bit deeply into the flesh of his palms,
then he forced himself to relax. An angry man was often a
rash man and he would require all of his wits about him if
he was to see this chore through. Swinging lithely into the
saddle, he turned, held up a hand to the girl, saw her lift
her own in reply. Then he touched spurs to the horse's
flanks and rode out of the courtyard. Fifteen minutes later,
the low cluster of buildings was out of sight and he was
riding swiftly over the rim of the valley with the harsh glare
of sunlight in his eyes.

He had covered three-quarters of the distance back to
town before there was any hint of trouble. It had been a long
and punishing ride across the blistering heat of the desert
and he felt the slackness in his horse and had thought of
stopping to allow it to get its wind when he picked up the
sound somewhere to his right. He rode on for a little while,
then reined up sharply on a low ledge of sandstone. The
wind, sweeping down from the hills far to the north, held an
inferno touch to its breath and brought with it a renewal of
the sound he had heard minutes before. He listened
intently, trying to identify it, knowing by some strange sense
deep within him that it was important he should do so. Like
the faintly ominous rumble of approaching thunder, it
rolled in waves of noise over the flat face of the desert, fading
at times to a mere whisper as the wind changed or slackened, then burgeoning up again, harsh and insistent.

Once or twice, he figured too that he heard the sharp
break of gunfire, superimposed on the overall rumble, but
it was not until he had progressed another mile that he
caught sight of the low, ominous dust cloud that lay
athwart the horizon, knew its meaning instantly with a
sudden chill of alarm. Sight and sound merged at once to
produce one single message for his brain.

Stampede!

Through the sun-hazed dust cloud he was able to make out the solid wall of flesh and horn and muscle that thundered across the plain and occasionally, a brief, tantalising glimpse of men on horseback, shooting into the air, urging the fear-crazed cattle onward. Short of a solid brick wall in their path, nothing was going to stop that thunderous herd until they had run themselves into the ground. For a long moment, Frank sat tall in the saddle, sucking in his lips, eyeing the mass of beef as they raced across his line of vision. At first, he failed to put two and two together and come up with the answer that was both obvious and spine-chilling. Those cattle were headed straight for Benton and there was no doubting whose they were, nor why they had been set on this particular course.

Foran had determined upon his own revenge for his humiliating loss of face in town the previous night. Frank had seen a town after it had been hit by stampeding cattle only once in his career, but it was an experience not readily erased from the mind. Even now, he doubted if there would be sufficient time for him to warn the unsuspecting inhabitants of their imminent danger.

Yet he had to try! He was in a position where he would come in sight of those men hazing that herd if he tried to head straight for town along the main trail, but that was a risk he would have to take. To skirt around them through the hills would take far too long. With a sharp intake of breath he brought down the rowels of his spurs hard, sorry for the horse as he did so, but knowing he had no other choice than to push the animal to its utmost limit. Fortunately the bay was a thoroughbred, otherwise he would never make it. The horse jumped into a run, its head down, ears flattened, shoes striking hard on the sun-baked earth.

Ahead of him, a ragged burst of shots rang out and he heard the sharp, high-pitched yells of the men. Dust eddied and swirled about him as he broke along the forward edge of the herd. Frank's heels drove hard against his horse's flanks as it raced alongside the fringe of crazed beasts. Long horns swung dangerously close. The needle-sharp tip of one grazed along Frank's thigh but he paid it no heed.

Pushing his sight through the dust that choked and enveloped him, he caught sight of one of the riders, looming out of the haze. The other closed his mouth with a snap as he recognized Frank, then opened it again to yell a warning to his companions. Without pausing, Frank urged his mount straight at the other, tugging the Colt from its holster. As he drew alongside the man, he raised his arm, brought the heavy butt crashing down on the man's skull. Without a sound the other toppled out of the saddle. There was no time to see whether or not he had fallen into the path of the onrushing herd. Tight packed and pounding along together, their wide horns almost locked into a net, the great beasts surged at him in a great tide, a living sea of monstrous flesh. A quick glance told him that the few precious seconds he had wasted with the gunman had lost the chance of getting clear of the forward swing of the stampede unless he did something drastic. Aiming deliberately, he put a slug between the eyes of the lead bull, dropped it in a threshing heap. The animals immediately behind continued to come on, some stumbling over the body, others swinging around it. For a few moments, however, their forward rush had been impeded. Grit clogged his mouth and throat, suffocating him. The throbbing roar behind his temples was a thunder almost equal to that of the herd. His eyes bulged from their sockets until the pressure was almost unbearable. He leaned forward, blinking in an effort to clear his eyeballs of the grit that rasped over them, threatening to blind him. His mount was now cutting its way obliquely across the forward rim of the herd and more than holding its own. Out of the edge of his vision, he had a picture of great, bobbing heads and staring eyes that filled his entire world; that and the ever-present dust which was still thickening in the air.

Coughing and gasping for air, he crouched over his horse's neck as it ran and it was this that saved him, for the slug that whined over his body just nicked his neck, bringing a faint trail of blood oozing from the narrow burn. He winced, risked a quick look over his shoulder, saw the man who had just ridden out of the dust. Jerking the Colt around, he loosed off a quick shot, missed, then lowered the gun as a surging bunch of steers split off from the main bulk and came between the rider and himself, cutting off his view of the other.

A second slug whined after him as he finally broke free of the path of the herd, but with the increasing range and his mount's swaying motion, he knew that it would take far better marksmen than these men to gun him down with revolvers. Ahead of him, he noticed the trail he was on ran through a narrow cleft between high rocks and he felt a shock of surprise as he noticed the man standing on an out-thrusting ledge of sandstone. the rifle already lifted to his shoulder, working the ejector with an ill-concealed haste. Frank snapped two shots at him. The first splashed rock within a foot of the other's leg, the second hit the stock of the rifle, sending it spinning from his grasp. Five seconds later, Frank was riding through the narrow canyon.

5

Gunsight

Barely fifteen minutes ahead of the approaching stampede, Frank rode into Renton. The main street was crowded with people. Several glanced round in surprise as he raced along the dusty street. There was no time for any individual warnings. Somewhere close behind him. countless tons of beef and muscle were headed for this spot; lunging, bellowing, fear-crazed beasts, knowing nothing but the savage urge to blunder forward in a straight and undeviating line, smashing down everything that stood in their way.

'Stampede!' He yelled the warning at the top of his lungs, noticed the sudden. startled looks on the faces of the people on the boardwalks. He pointed behind him to add urgency to his words. Then they began to scatter. In some mysterious way, the windows on either side of the street had filled within seconds. A woman hustled two children across the street behind Frank as he slid from the saddle on the run outside the sheriff's office, yelling for Talbot.

The other came running out at his call, a rifle in his hands. He looked up and down the street for a moment, his face apprehensive, then down at Frank.

'What is it?' he asked hoarsely. 'What's the trouble?'

'Foran's stampeded part of his herd out there. He's headed it for the town. We've got to get everybody off the streets, and the horses before all of that beef hits town.'

'Hell.' The other swore sharply. He propped the rifle against the wooden upright. Running as swiftly as his legs would carry him, he ran along the street, waving his arms and yelling at any of the bystanders still out in the open. Within minutes, the town seemed miraculously cleared of life. Only Frank and Talbot remained on the street waiting for the unmistakable thunder of hooves to herald the approach of the stampede.

'Anythin' we can do to stop 'em?' Talbot asked harshly. As yet there was no evidence of the disaster which threatened. 'Maybe set up a barricade at the end of the street. It might divide most of 'em before they get into town.'

Frank was dubious about this, having seen those steers on the run, but it did give them something of a chance, particularly if they could get a few men with rifles crouched behind it to drop some of the natural leaders of that herd.

Nodding, he said sharply: 'Try to get some men together. Tell them to bring guns. We may be able to turn 'em, but there isn't much time. Another ten minutes and they'll be here, racing through the main street.' He shivered at the thought of all the tremendous damage which a thousand head of beef on the move could do to a town such as this which stood in their path.

Working against time, with every second precious, they hauled wagons across the road at the very edge of town where low-roofed shanties led off to right and left of the street, forming a natural dividing point if only they could succeed in dropping the leaders and slowing the rest before they crashed through the barricade they were erecting.

Talbot had wasted no time. Getting ten men together,

they hauled and tugged the wagons and lengths of fencing into place. By the time they had finished, the thunder of the oncoming herd was clearly audible in the distance and through the twisted bars of metal and wood, they were able to make out the dust smoke that marked its position.

'Everybody in position and knows what to do?' Frank called loudly. He turned to glance in both directions at the men crouched down behind the barricade, their weapons at the ready, their faces grim, beaded with sweat and grimed with dirt. They nodded, steadied their weapons, shoulders hunched forward, the muscles of their faces working with the strain of waiting.

'Hell,' muttered Talbot again. 'If this don't work out, Frank, we're liable to find ourselves smashed to pulp under those hooves.'

'You think that thought hasn't already occurred to me?' Frank grunted. 'I've been thinkin' of nothing else.' Lying there, he tried to forget the aches and bruises in his limbs. The lack of sleep was beginning to take its toll of him too and it was increasingly difficult to concentrate.

Drawing himself together, he forced his gaze through the dust smoke that rolled ominously towards the town. The thunder of hooves grew louder in his ears. Less than four hundred yards away now – three hundred. Watching the inexorable approach of the stampeding herd, Frank wondered briefly if anything on earth possessed the power to stop it. Their guns were pitifully few to make any impression on that wall of muscle. It was a highly dangerous moment. The first of the steers was less than a hundred and fifty yards away when he yelled harshly: 'Open fire! Aim for the leaders.'

A ragged volley of gunfire rang out, the sound almost lost in the roar of hooves. Frank aimed carefully in contrast to the others who were blazing away frenziedly, fear driving them. He saw one of the leading bulls go down on to its knees as the heavy bullet took it between the eyes. It vanished at once under the onrushing tide of flesh which engulfed it, obliterated it within seconds. To Frank it seemed inevitable that the stampede urge was too strong within the animals and they would keep up their headlong plunge unchecked.

Volley after volley crashed into the surging animals but with no visible effect, with no slowing of their forward, hammering run. Then, sweating from nervous exhaustion, he cringed at a sudden cavernous explosion that came from directly in front of him. Debris showered on to his prone body as he flung up a hand in front of his eyes in an attempt to shield his face. Seconds passed before he realized what had happened. On the boardwalk, right at the very end of the hastily thrown-up barricade, Herb Forrest, grinning toothlessly, had hurled a home-made bomb at the oncoming herd, a couple of fused sticks of dynamite tied together. Simple, but highly effective as it proved. Bellowing and plunging in frantic fear, the leading wave split, surging on either side of the wrinkle-edged crater which had been blown out of the dirt.

The guns in the hands of the men crouched low behind the wagons splashed more flame, turning the cattle from their original direction, sending them scattering to either side. But now the men faced a new danger. Return fire spat at them as the riders, moving in along the curving flanks of the stampeding herd, opened up. Foiled in their original intention, they still meant to take some of the Benton men with them. Crouching low over the necks of their mounts, they raced towards the barrier, firing as they came. One of the men next to Frank uttered a low, coughing moan, reeled back with a bullet in his shoulder, one hand up to his chest, blood trickling between his rigid fingers.

Frank lifted his own gun, aimed high at the rider looming over him as the other attempted to put his mount over the tongue of the wagon. The bullet nicked the man's neck, drew blood. He swayed in the saddle, hung on desperately with his knees as his mount reared suddenly, threatening to unseat him. The next moment, horse and rider had cleared the wagon tongue and, acting on instinct, Frank rose swiftly to his feet, caught the man by the arm and dragged him off the running horse. A revolver boomed from somewhere nearby and lead ricocheted off the ground between Frank's feet. Then they were both on the ground, the gunman straining to bring the barrel of his Colt in line with Frank's chest, his finger hard on the trigger. The grin that twisted his lips into a cruel line reflected all of the hatred and bestiality there was in his malicious nature.

For a moment, the gun was dead centre of Frank's chest and the outlaw grinned more widely, evidently enjoying his moment of mastery; but it was a moment over which he had lingered a little too long. A steer suddenly crashed into the side of the wagon, a fear-crazed animal that had broken from the main mass of the herd and pursued its forward rush. The animal ran into Frank's opponent from the side, knocked his arm around and the bullet merely grazed his shoulder instead of going plumb through his heart. Before the Colt could blast again, Frank grabbed at the other's wrists, thrust them back with a surge of super-human strength, knowing that the other would not miss a second time. Before the man could steady himself, he kicked upward with his feet into the gunhawk's stomach, heaved and rolled in the same motion, twisting the man over his head, to land with a dull thud in the dust a few feet behind.

Swiftly, Frank grubbed in the dust for the gun which had dropped from his fist, determined to drop the other before he could collect his stunned senses; but when he turned his head, he saw that such a move was not necessary. The man lay where he had fallen, unmoving. Shaking his head to clear it, Frank crawled over to him, turned him over, then withdrew his hand sharply as he felt the sticky warmth of blood on his fingers. Easing the other up, he saw where the man had fallen heavily on the upthrusting stake, knew he had died instantly. Lowering the gunhawk to the floor. he turned back to the barricade. The Double Circle riders had fanned out now, were crouched down behind the broken-down shacks, half hidden in the swirling dust cloud of the drag where the remnants of the fleeing herd were disappearing into the distance around the perimeter of the town. There was no longer any real danger from the stampede apart from a handful of steers that had jumped the wagons and were racing pell-mell along the street, scattering a few of the townsfolk who had came out to see what was going on.

Frank studied the terrain through narrowed eyes. As far as he could judge, ten men were hidden behind the shanties in well-concealed positions from which they could lay a barrage of fire across the end of the street without exposing themselves overmuch to return fire.

'We've got to get our fire at their rear and flanks if we're to do any damage,' he said decisively. He looked to either side. The dust still hung heavy and thick in the air and would afford them a little cover. 'We'll set up two men here, behind the wagons to afford us coverin' fire. Sheriff – when they cut loose, you take three of the men and cut low into the alley yonder, which should bring you out to the side of the shanties and above them. The rest of us will swing around to the left.' He saw the men nod, albeit a little reluctantly. They had been brought into this affair merely to stand by the barricade and try to prevent a stampeding herd from sweeping unchecked into a defenceless town and wreaking terrible damage. Now they were being asked to do the one thing they had always shied at in the past – go up against Witney Foran's professional gunmen.

'You want I should use another couple of these sticks of dynamite, Marshal?' asked Forrest, still grinning. The oldster appeared to be thoroughly enjoying himself in stark contrast to the others.

Frank cast a practised glance in the direction of the nearest shack, then shook his head. 'Much too far, old-timer,' he affirmed. 'Even I couldn't hit that hut from here.'

'Could be one of us might get close enough,' suggested Talbot, squinting through the enshrouding dust.

'It's possible.' He looked round at Forrest. 'Get a couple of those bombs ready, Herb. We'll take 'em with us. If we do get a chance to use 'em, it might turn things in our favour.'

When the sticks of dynamite were ready, he nodded to the two men who were to remain behind the wagons. 'Get set to chop those places to matchwood,' he said tightly. 'Everybody just remember. Those *hombres* out there are workin' to orders from Foran. If we don't beat 'em here and now, we may never get another chance to hit him as hard as this. OK, get movin'.'

Rapidly conceived, the plan was just as quickly put into action. But like so many plans it did not go through without some errors. The vicious bellow of the covering fire was the signal for the two groups of men to rush for the comparative safety of the narrow alleys on either side of the street. Frank scuttled across, keeping behind the wagons laid across the entrance as far as possible, hearing the waspish hum of lead striking all around him as the Double Circle men opened up. Slugs ripped along the walls of the nearby buildings, smashed through windows just above his head as he flung himself headlong into the dirt for the last ten feet, his chest striking the ground hard, legs doubling up as more gunfire smashed into the earth behind him. A ricochet whined off a wall, hummed dangerously close to his head as he wriggled forward. Moments later, the other men joined him, but the last man across never made it. A savage, blustering hail of lead struck his body, spun him violently around while he was still five feet from safety and pitched him sprawling on to his face. His body twitched convulsively for a few seconds, then became still.

Thrusting himself to his feet, Frank gestured the others to follow him, knowing the reason for their sudden hesitation as they stared with wide-open eyes at the dead man lying in the street.

'Just keep moving!' he ordered harshly. 'If you give up now, we'll all be just as dead as he is.'

Somehow, his words got through to their frightened brains. They followed him automatically, faces twisted into tight, grim masks. The men behind the barrier were still pouring a hail of shots into the flimsy wooden walls of the shanties, but their fire seemed to be giving the men there little trouble so far. Gasping dust-laden air down into his tortured lungs, scarcely able to make out anything through the haze, Frank staggered to the end of the alley, pressed his body close to the wall as he risked a quick look around the corner of the abandoned grain store at the very end. From where he stood, it was just possible to make out the legs and bottom half of a man's body where he lay on his stomach behind an inverted rain barrel, some thirty yards away. He could see nothing of the other Double Circle rannies, but the steadily increasing volume of gunfire told him that, for the most part, they were still unhurt and securely concealed.

Motioning the other men forward, he waited until they had taken up their positions. In his left hand. he held the homemade bomb, the short length of fuse dangling from between the two sticks of dynamite. It needed only the touch of a match to the end of that innocent-looking fuse to blow an entire shanty to pieces, destroying most of the men who lay behind it.

'It's not goin' to be easy to get within range, Marshal,' said one of the men tightly. 'It's open ground from here on in and they could pick you off before you'd gone a couple of paces.'

Frank drew his eyes down tight, brow furrowed. The other was right in one respect at least. The ground between them and the nearest shack was completely open without the smallest scrap of cover. Even if he did succeed in getting close enough to heave the dynamite on target, he would himself be in danger from the blast and flying debris. But it was a risk he had to take. There was no other choice left open to him. The breeze thinned the dust and blue-hazed gunsmoke for a moment. Through the gap, he saw two of the gunslingers rise to their feet, run back from the rear of the wooden hut.

'They're retreatin',' called one of the men, pointing. He jerked up his Colt, loosed off five shots in rapid succession, the bullets kicking up spurts of dust around the running men. Both dropped out of sight into a low hollow, and it was impossible to tell if either had been hit by the sporadic fire.

'Hold your fire,' Frank commanded. 'They're not pullin' out, just movin' to better positions where they can sight on any man movin' towards the shacks. Could be they've divined our intentions.'

'What do we do then, Marshal?' muttered another man, peering into the haze. 'There must be five or six still holed up near that shack and with those two back there, it would be suicide to try anythin'.'

'Maybe. Maybe not.' Frank sucked in his lips. If he could only reach that depression and take care of the two men in it, it would provide him with the cover he needed.

'Stay here,' he ordered. 'I'll handle this.'

'Don't be a goddamn fool, Marshal,' said the first man. 'You don't have a chance in hell.' But he was already talking to the empty air, for Frank had gone, running lightly over the uneven ground on the balls of his feet, gripping the explosive in one hand, the Colt in the other. He had covered half the distance to the hollow before there was any gunfire directed at him. His sudden move had taken the men completely by surprise. Using a bobbing, weaving gait to make himself a more difficult target to hit, he heard bullets hum their song of death all around him. Something invisible plucked at the sleeve of his jacket, but he forced himself to ignore it. Accelerating rapidly, forcing his legs to obey him, he came upon the lip of the depression.

Both men saw him in the same instant. He had time to notice the look of stunned surprise on their faces before the Colt in his right hand belched flame and lead. The nearer man fell back with a hole between his eyes, his gun jetting aimlessly into the air, the bullet driving past Frank's shoulder as he flung himself down beside the other. The man uttered a grunt of agony. as Frank's booted foot caught him full in the midriff, knocking the air from his body. But even as he fell, he twisted catlike on the ground, kicking upward in a savage attempt to kill or maim. The toecap of his boot caught Frank on the left kneecap and he felt his legs go from under him. Seizing his momentary advantage, the gunman swung his arm, aiming to smash in Frank's skull with the butt of his Colt. Only the swift sideways movement of his head saved Frank at that moment. Nevertheless, the gunbutt struck him a glancing blow on the scalp, half stunning him, knocking him back against the sandy wall of the depression. Desperately he fought to retain a hold on his swiftly buckling senses, his vision blurring, pain and thunder roaring through his brain.

Grinning fiercely, the gunhawk thumped another blow at him, thrusting himself up on to his feet as he did so, standing on straddled legs as he strove to sight the gun in his hand on Frank's chest. Drawing himself together for one last tremendous effort, Frank kicked out with both feet, hitting the man in the chest, toppling him backward. The other's Colt roared once as the gunhawk's finger pressed the trigger but the bullet went wild as his back-falling motion carried his gun arm sharply upward.

Frank hurled himself forward and up. He caught at the pistol, wresting it from the owner's grasp as it roared a second time. Then he smashed his fist into the man's stomach, felt him cave in under the force of the blow, doubling up so that his knees almost touched his chin. Gripping the other's shirt, he hauled him up off the floor of the depression, raised the butt of the sixgun he had snatched from his opponent and struck hard and quick at the man's exposed neck. The gunslinger fell back without a single bleat of sound. The chances were that the shocking impact of the blow had snapped his neck like a rotten twig. Anyway, he would be out cold for long enough, if he wasn't already dead.

Drawing breath into his heaving lungs in harsh gasps that threatened to tear his bruised, battered body in half, he raised his head cautiously, peered through the low lying haze of blue gunsmoke. The gunfight was still in progress and it was soon evident that the townsmen were getting the worst of it. So far, it seemed, no reinforcements had appeared to give them a hand and the bunch of men led by Sheriff Talbot were pinned down behind a line of wooden barrels, unable to move in any direction without exposing themselves to intense and highly accurate fire.

At the moment, however, none of the Double Circle attackers appeared to be taking overmuch notice of what had happened to their rear. All seemed to be occupied in pouring fire into the barricade and the mouths of the alleys where they opened out on to the open ground around the perimeter of the town.

Reaching into the loose sand at his back, he found the sticks of dynamite with the fuse fortunately still in position. Bending, he struck a match, applied the flame to the exposed end of the fuse, waited for a moment while it began to splutter, then drew back his arm and threw it in a high lob towards the low wooden building less than twenty feet away. He watched as the small bundle arced through the hazy air, saw it land within a few inches of one of the crouching men, saw the man turn his head sharply at the faint sound. It was impossible to make out the look on the man's face as he recognized the bundle for what it was, but he was just able to catch a fragmentary glimpse of the other rearing wildly to his knees, a yell bursting from his lips. Then Frank had pulled his head down, his arms over it. The blast, when it came, sounded oddly muffled, but as he lifted his head to peer over the lip of the hollow, he saw the tremendous sheet of flame which had suddenly engulfed the ramshackle building with smoke mushrooming above the spot where it had been. Long, flickering tongues of red-edged flame licked among the tumbled debris and twisted pieces of wood and planking were still raining down all about him.

Yells of terror went up from the remaining Double Circle men. Frank was still on his knees when they burst forth from their place of concealment and ran for their horses. He triggered off a couple of shots after them, saw one man reel and clutch at his shoulder just as he reached his mount. Before Frank could send another shot at him, one of his companions, already mounted, raced past, caught the wounded man by the arm and swung him up into the saddle behind him. Two minutes later, the fight was all over.

Clawing himself out of the hollow, Frank moved slowly forward, gun in hand, but there was no more shooting. The town seemed suddenly deathly quiet. Talbot strode from behind the barrels. He stood for a moment looking around at the scene of destruction, then shrugged his shoulders philosophically.

'Reckon it could've been a sight worse,' he grunted, rubbing a dirty white handkerchief over his glistening forehead. It came away streaked with dust and a thin smear of blood from a deep gash over his left eye. 'Goddamn! If I ain't been hit and I never knew a thing.'

'Nothin' more'n a scratch,' Frank told him. He thrust the Colt back into its holster. 'Guess we can take down that barricade now. Foran won't try anythin' with Benton again for a while, I reckon.'

Talbot gave a brief nod, motioned to a few of the watching men. While they were engaged in removing the wagons, he and Frank made their way back along the street to the jail. Now that the excitement was over for the time being, Frank could scarcely suppress the deep-seated weariness that surged through his body in an enervating wave of fatigue.

'You look all tuckered in, Marshal,' said Talbot. He brought out the bottle of whiskey. 'Better get a little of this inside you. Make you feel a mite better. Anyways, I figure you've deserved it after that little fracas.'

Frank nodded, tossed the liquor back in a single gulp. 'Could be that it'll show the other ranchers that we are capable of standin' up to Foran when we try,' he muttered thickly. His lips seemed to be swollen to twice their normal size and there was a burning pain in his chest and another area of agony down the side of his scalp where the gunman's heavy weapon had struck him that glancing blow.

'Foran will have a job on his hands roundin' up all those cattle of his.' Talbot sat back, put his legs out on top of the desk, pushed his hat further back on his head. He seemed to have gained a lot in confidence over the past twenty-four hours, Frank thought, looking at him. Maybe this was what he needed to make him feel a man again. For much of his time as sheriff in the past couple of years he had been dominated by Foran and his men, jumping at their beck and call. Now he had turned, had regained his manhood.

'How's your prisoner been behavin' himself while I've been away?'

Talbot grinned. 'Reckon he's resigned himself to the

fact that he's goin' to stand trial and that Foran won't be in a position to help him.' The other drew a cigar from his pocket, thrust it between his fleshy lips. 'I sure wish that Fentry would show up, though. It makes me kinda nervous having that hombre in that cell back there. He's as much a rattler as the rest of that bunch and I sure do get the feelin' now and again, that he'll make an effort to break out on his lonesome if Foran doesn't do somethin' soon.'

'Guess it might cool him off some if we were to tell him about this latest episode.' He got to his feet, picked the bunch of keys off the wall behind the desk and went along to the cells at the rear of the building. Blackie Carron was seated on the low bunk against one wall. He glanced up as Frank stood at the door, looking in at him.

'Heard some shootin' out there a while ago, Marshal,' he said, grinning. 'That's just a taste of what'll happen when Foran really starts.'

'Guess he's already tried,' Frank said evenly. 'So far, he ain't made much of a job of it.'

The other's eyes narrowed. For a moment, he seemed at a loss for words, then the sneering grin returned to his face. 'You can't bluff me like that, Condor. Foran can smash this town whenever he feels like it.' A cunning look spread over his face. 'You ever seen a town that's been braced by a trail crew? They'll put it to the torch and once a fire is started in a place like this, it'll all go up like tinder.'

'Guess they've got to get here first before they can make any trouble.' Frank leaned nonchalantly against the cell door, rolled a smoke. 'Better make up your mind right now, Carron. Foran won't help you now. He's got too many other problems of his own to keep him occupied; real big problems. He tried to stampede his herd through the town a while back, sent several of his boys with it, just to make sure. More'n half of 'em are dead right now and as for the Double Circle herd, the best part of it is scattered over fifty square miles of prairie.'

'That won't hold him for long,' asserted Carron. 'Just wait and see. You're just foolin' yourselves if you think this is the finish. For you it's only the beginning.'

'You talk too damn much,' Frank said. 'Once you've been tried and found guilty, reckon there won't be much talk left in you.'

The other heaved himself to his feet, stepped forward, big hands grasping the bars. He thrust his bearded face close to Frank's. 'I've been doin' a whole heap of thinkin' about that, Marshal,' he gritted. 'How come Judge Fentry ain't shown up yet to start the trial? You've been spoutin' off about it ever since I got locked away in this cell. Reckon if he was all that anxious to do it, he'd have been here by now. Come to gloat.'

'He'll be here when he's good and ready.' Frank did not remove his gaze from the other as he spoke, yet it was difficult not to suppress entirely the wave of apprehension that swept through him at the other's casual remark. Just how much did the foreman suspect? Pretty soon, the rest of the townsfolk would be asking themselves the very same question. With an effort, he put the thought out of his mind, turned on his heel, calling over his shoulder. 'I'll see you get somethin' to eat, Carron. We don't want you starvin' on us before we hitch a riata around that neck of yours.'

Witney Foran was in an ugly mood. It showed in his face and his manner as he stood in front of the window, staring out at the horses which milled around restlessly in the big corral. Behind him, Frisco felt a sudden stab of anger. When the other did not break the silence which had existed between them for more than five minutes, he said tartly, 'I don't see why the hell you should blame me for that fiasco in town. I had nothin' to do with the whole affair, was against it from the start. But you had to listen to the Maceys. They were both so all-fired sure they could stampede that herd through Benton and smash down everythin' in their way.'

Foran swung quickly on his heel, glared across the room at the gunfighter. 'The idea was sound enough,' he blazed. 'It just happened that Condor spotted the herd on the move and managed to get through and warn the town. Otherwise, Benton would have been flattened by now.'

'So once again, we've failed to eliminate Condor. Seems to me that this bastard of a Marshal has got in our hair once too often. You ought to have called his bluff when we rode in to free Carson.'

'You think that damnfool sheriff wouldn't have pressed the triggers of that scattergun he was holdin'? It would have given him just the excuse he'd been waitin' for. He's a coward, there's no denyin' that, and he got some odd notion that it ain't right to kill a man unless you can do it all perfectly legal. But on that occasion, he'd have done it with a clear conscience. I didn't see you ready to call him out, especially with Condor behind us with a gun.'

'Sooner or later, Condor and me are goin' to meet face to face and then we'll see who's got the fastest gun,' snarled Frisco.

Foran's face remained grim. 'I wouldn't be too damn sure you can take him,' he said deliberately. 'He ain't like the ordinary run of marshals. He's wizard fast with a gun.' He smashed his clenched fist hard on the table. 'But nevertheless, I want him dead – and I want it done fast. With no more mistakes. So long as he's alive and kickin', he's a menace.'

Frisco hitched his gunbelt a little higher around his middle. For a moment there was a little devil leaping at the back of the dark eyes, a feral glow that sent a shiver through Foran's body. It was the crazed look of a killer, something he had seen, not once, but several times before and it meant death for somebody.

'You givin' me the chance to take Condor in my own

way, without any interference from the Macey's?' Frisco
asked pertinently.

An air of strict guarded attention to fact came over
Foran. The earlier fury of the day which had come when
word had arrived of the failure of the plan to smash
Benton and the loss of six of his men had settled somewhat inside him to a black and implacable hatred of Frank
Condor. The man had been a thorn in his side for too
long, he decided. Everything was boiling around within
his mind, giving him no peace, no chance to remake his
plans and think ahead. Condor was deliberately pushing
him to the brink of savage and rash action and he knew
only too well that this way could conceivably lead to
absolute disaster. He picked up the whiskey bottle from
the table, poured a drink without offering one to the
other and drank it in short, avid gulps.

'All right,' he muttered finally. 'If you reckon you can
take him, ride into Benton and finish the job tonight.'

'And Blackie? You want him out of jail once I've
finished that particular chore?'

'Sure. Bring him back here. He's a good man and I
need him. Once Condor is dead, we'll ride against Carson.
With him out of the way, I can take over the rest of the
land at my leisure without any trouble.'

'Condor has been tryin' to work up the other ranchers
into throwin' in their lot with him. I suppose you know
that already?'

Foran nodded. 'I've got my ways of findin' out what
goes on in Benton. There's very little I don't know. Now
you'd better dust along if you're to get to town by
sundown. Want any of the boys to go along with you?'

'Nope. I figure this is somethin' I'll do best on my own.'
He took out the Colts one at a time, spun the chambers
smoothly checking that they were both fully loaded, then
pouched them again. 'No need to worry none. Condor
will be buzzard bait by mornin'.'

Leaving the ranch house, he went over to the corral, roped out his mount and threw a saddle on to the horse, tightening the cinch under the animal's belly, checking the Winchester, before swinging up in a smooth motion. He raised his hand in mock salute to Foran as he rode out in a cloud of slowly-settling dust.

After he had gone, two shadows detached themselves from the barn and walked over to Foran, their spurs dragging dust. Pausing in front of the rancher, Flint Macey said brusquely: 'Just saw Frisco ride out in a powerful hurry, Foran. He got some urgent business to settle?'

'That's right.' The other gave a curt nod. After what had happened over the past day, he was now beginning to wonder whether he had done the right thing in bringing these two killers up from Texas to work for him. They were both ruthless killers, it was true, the breed of men he had been looking for to back his plans. But he also had the feeling that they were not the sort of men who willingly took to accepting orders and he felt a little uneasy whenever they were around.

'His business in Benton, maybe?' inquired Clay tonelessly. There was something in his voice which implied more than a casual interest.

'Maybe.' Foran stiffened. 'But when I give him orders, he carries them out. I expect that loyalty from every man on my payroll, no matter what his own opinions might be or whether he had some personal interest in the matter.'

'Meanin' what?'

'Just that while you've been here I've had the feelin' that there's something on your minds concernin' Frank Condor. Whatever it is – forget it! He's my problem and I'll get rid of him in any way I think fit.'

'And you've sent Frisco into town to eliminate that particular problem.' It was more of a statement than a question.

'Yes.'

The other scratched his chin. There was a belligerent note to his harsh voice as he said: 'I always figured you brought us here to do that particular chore for you. Seems I was mistaken.'

'You got any grouse with Condor?'

The other said nothing for a long moment, then shrugged. 'Reckon you might as well know it. Me and my brother were teamed up with a *hombre* named Condor coupla years ago, down Texas way. This kid was Frank Condor's brother, turned back. He reckoned that with him alongside us, we could figure the marshal out of any deals we made. Weren't likely he'd make a play for his own brother.'

'And—?' prompted Foran interestedly as the other paused to light a quirly.

Macey blew smoke into the air. He spoke through it thinly, with a voice edged by anger. 'Guess we had him figured all wrong. We'd stuck up this bank in town. No trouble at all. Just as we were pullin' out, the marshal appears on the scene, called on us to throw down our guns. Young Condor wasn't havin' any, pulled on his brother. It was a damnfool thing to do anyway. Frank Condor shot him down like he was any other outlaw. We only managed to escape by the skin of our teeth. Young Condor had the money in his saddlebags, so we lost it all.'

'So that's why Condor lit out of Texas and headed this way, why he put his guns away,' mused Foran speculatively. He furrowed his brow. A lot of things were making sense now, things which he had not previously understood about the tall lawman.

'And that's why we want him. When he dies, I want him to know we did it – and why. That's why I don't cotton on to this idea of yours sendin' Frisco after him.'

'All right, so it's done now. Maybe if you'd spoken up sooner about this, things could've been different. Far as I'm concerned, so long as he's dead, it doesn't matter who kills him; so long as they get him out of my hair. He's been talkin' to the other ranchers hereabouts, stirrin' 'em up. Could mean trouble for me if he gets his way.'

Macey dragged deeply on his smoke. 'You skeert of them?' Naked sarcasm edged his tone.

'Not scared. But I don't want to lose more men than I need. If I could pick 'em off one at a time, there'd be no trouble.'

'Then why not hit 'em now, before they're ready? No sense in givin' them time to prepare. Let me have a dozen men and I'll take 'em all for you.'

Foran pondered that for a moment. In the heat of all that had happened over the last few days, it was a possibility which he had overlooked. Certainly it made sense. Finally, he nodded. 'All right. Start tonight. I suggest you ride out to the Lazy L ranch, run by a fella named Credin. It borders this spread to the north on a bend of the Red.'

'This fella Credin may object,' grinned Macey evilly. 'Kinda hope that he does. Things have been pretty tame around here since we arrived in spite of the excitement you promised us.'

'They're liable to hot up soon,' Foran promised. 'Maybe sooner than you think. Credin isn't a pushover by any means and he'll have been alerted by Condor.'

'I'll keep that in mind.' Macey nodded. He gave a smothered laugh, turned on his heel and walked insolently back to the bunkhouse. Foran watched him go with a slight shiver. He was used to having killers around him, had been forced to rely on their help to get where he was and he thought he knew every type. But these two men were different from any others he had ever known. Soulless, utterly ruthless, caring less than nothing for human life. He figured he could forget about Credin and his crew after that night.

There was a low moon swinging above the Red River as Flint and Clay Macey rode out of the Double Circle ranch at the head of a group of gunhawks. They rode through the narrow cut of a long-dry creek towards a tall stand of oak and scrub. Now that they were set for some killing and burning, Flint Macey was filled with a strangely heightened anticipation. This was not the first time he had ridden out on a night mission such as this and the sly fox of eager exhilaration in his brain kept whispering: '*Burn! Destroy!*'

On either side of them. the thick brush which grew along the banks of the creek sheltered them from the icy wind that rustled the stiff stems of the sage with a harsh crackling sound. Down here, too, they were protected from the chance view of anybody in the country above and that was the way he wanted it. He wanted to hit the Lazy L spread without warning. Anyway, who was there up above to see or hear them? The whole vast stretch of the country around them was deathly, almost ghostly, silent. At the end of the creek bed, he pulled up and listened intently, motioning the others to be quiet. Macey was not a superstitious man, but he did not like anything connected with ghosts to move into his thoughts. He had probably killed more men in his lifetime than most other gunmen, not only through the war, but since. Now, sometimes, in spite of his efforts to erase these memories from his mind, things came back to remind him of his victims. The wind in the brush was now a constant reminder of the cries of the men and women he had shot down without mercy and he did not like it.

'You hear somethin'?' Clay edged his mount forward until he drew level with his brother.

'Nothin' but the wind,' growled the other harshly. He tugged hard on the reins. 'Let's go.'

For a while, the trail led them through a series of depressions, across bare ground with only an occasional stunted tree as a landmark. Then, as they turned their mounts and swung north, they rode along the narrow strip of ground, covered with mesquite and Spanish Sword, which divided the Double Circle spread from the Lazy L.

It was bad ground, especially as far as the horses were concerned. The razor-edged Spanish Sword cut at their feet until they were slashed and bloody. But it was the one approach to the Lazy L ranch which Credin would not think of guarding, simply because it was virtually suicidal for men to try to push their mounts through these terrible growths.

'Hell,' swore Clay as his horse stumbled. 'This ain't no trail at all. Why can't we just ride in and put a torch to the place like we used to do in the old days?'

'We'll do that soon enough,' snapped the other. 'Now keep your voice down. We'll be on the Lazy L spread any minute now if Foran is right, the ranch ain't far from the boundary markers.'

'It can't be near enough for me,' grunted the other. He lapsed into a sullen silence.

Ten minutes later, they ran into barbed wire stretched across the trail. Flint pushed his mount right up to it, so that the barbs touched his horse's chest. He stared down to where the cruel strands glinted faintly in the flooding moonlight. 'Reckon that Credin don't trust our new boss none too much. Guess he's got some real cause.' He jogged the horse a few yards to one side, wound the loop of his riata securely around the top of the post, fastened the other end to his saddle horn and kicked savagely with his rowels at the animal's flanks, causing it to rear upward and back, dragging the rope taut. Another touch of the spurs, a further backward tug and the post came up from the ground, the wire collapsing in both directions.

In single file, they made their way through the gap in the boundary fence, rode across a low hill, covered with lush grass that grew along the bank of the Red River. It was good cattle country, Flint admitted. He could guess why Foran wanted it all so badly. If a man owned all of this land, he would be extremely powerful indeed, well able to fight off any of the settlers when any of the nesters moved in on Government grants. It had happened before. These squatters obtained grants from the Government in Washington giving them claim to much of the land which the ranchers believed to be theirs by right of prior occupation and only the really big men were sufficiently strong to retain their hold on the range. Clearly, Foran intended to be one of those men, no matter what happened to the others.

Topping a rise, they came within sight of the ranch house. It lay at the end of a long valley, within hailing distance of the river which moved wide and sluggish at this point. Whoever had originally built that ranch had certainly picked the best spot for it, Macey thought grudgingly. Then the little voice of hate began muttering in his brain once more, setting it afire.

They put their horses to the slope, fanning out. They slid from their saddles on the edge of the courtyard, their guns out as they ran for cover. Macey scanned either side of the cluster of buildings. It wasn't likely that Credin would leave the place entirely unguarded, but at the moment he could see no sign of any of the Lazy L crew and it was doubtful if any look-out would have allowed them to get so close without giving a warning shot to alert the others.

'Reckon we must've hit 'em at the right moment,' grunted one of the men.

'Could be,' Flint agreed. He still looked straight ahead but the corners of his mouth twisted up a little and he thumbed back the hammer of his Colt.

'Somebody comin' over that way,' murmured Clay tightly. He pointed with the barrel of his sixgun.

The solitary rider had approached from the far side of the ranch, riding down the grassy hill, which explained why they had not heard his approach. The man was almost at the house, had just slid from his saddle, was reaching up to take the long-barrelled Winchester from its scabbard, when Flint hissed tightly:

'*Get him!*'

In a split second. Clay had lifted his gun and three shots rattled out, the echoes of them blending into a single blur of sound. The rider reeled as the shots hammered home into his body, then straightened, jerked back behind the horse and levelled the Winchester. He loosed off only one shot, with the last ounce of strength left in his trigger finger, but by some freak of chance, the slug found its mark and the man close beside Flint swayed back with a coughing grunt, hand clutching at his chest, the blood spurting from his mouth with every spluttering exhalation as he toppled sideways.

Within seconds pandemonium broke loose. Less than a quarter of a minute after the first shots, guns were firing from the windows of the ranch house while others joined in from the bunkhouse and the barn nearby. A window shattered and even as Macey went down behind a piece of deadwood, three men rushed from the bunkhouse, flung themselves down behind the horse trough in the court-yard, ripping off shots as they did so.

'Spread out!' Flint roared at the top of his lungs, bellowing the order. Another man fell, but the rest ran, humped over, for the thin fringe of trees, ducking out of sight. Lead hummed viciously across the courtyard. In the corral, the horses whinneyed in fright, stampeded for the far corner.

'Most of the crew are in the bunkhouse,' muttered Clay, edging close. He let his gaze wander over the smooth slope which led down to it. 'Now if we was to get torches and fire it, the wind's just right to carry over to the ranch house.'

'OK, get goin'. We'll hold 'em off until you're ready.'

Clay scuttled away, calling to a couple of men to follow

him. Flint saw them dive out of sight into the trees, then turned his attention back to the gun battle, grinning wolfishly. A head lifted inquisitively above the edge of the water bough and Flint's Colt spat spitefully. The head dropped out of sight.

Now the volume of gunfire had shifted around towards the rear of the buildings where the rest of the Double Circle men had moved into position to cut off any escape from that direction. Credin and his crew were bottled up nicely. But the return fire had doubled in volume too and bullets rustled eerily through the grass all around him as he wriggled sideways into a fresh position.

What the hell was Clay doing, he wondered fiercely. The sooner they burned those men out, the better. Once they panicked them into the open it would be like shooting down sitting ducks. There was a rustle at his back and the three men came crawling down the slope, carrying the pine torches in their hands.

'All set?' Flint growled. 'They're gettin' powerful close with that lead.'

The other grinned, teeth showing whitely in his shadowed face. He nodded, leaned back on to his side and struck a match, setting light to the bundle of twigs and shavings. It sparked at once, flaming brilliantly.

'Give us some covering fire,' muttered the other hoarsely.

Flint punched fresh shells into the Colt, spun the chamber, then ripped off shot after shot, aiming for the door of the bunkhouse from which most of the fire was coming. The three men raced down the slope, flopped behind a rock, the flaring torches lighting their position. Lead crashed all about them and Flint saw one of the three stagger and fall, the torch dropping from his fingers. Within seconds, the dry grass was alight, fanned by the breeze. Clay and the other man hesitated for a moment then, as though recognizing the precariousness of their position, hurled their torches in twin blazing arcs at the bunkhouse. The first hit the side of the building, fell back on to the sun-baked earth, spluttering and throwing off a shower of sparks; but the second sailed through the open doorway, landing amid the straw piled high just inside the bunkhouse, obviously an overflow from the nearby barn.

Flint's primitive lust to kill was whipped to a frenzy of excitement by the sight of the licking flames which gained a firm hold within moments. As the fire leapt up to the roof of the building, burning with a fierce orange glow, he moved with the speed of a rattler, yelling to the others. Flinging himself forward, he reached the edge of the courtyard in a couple of bounds, the Colt jerking against his wrist as he triggered off a series of shots at the men who came tumbling out of the bunkhouse. He shot down three of them before they could return his fire. From inside the building there came the agonized yells of men trapped at the rear by the barrier of fire which now blocked the exit. Already, the flames had caught at the timber-dry roof and sparks were being carried across in the direction of the barn and the house itself as Clay had guessed they would.

Within minutes, the place was a scene of chaos, lit by the crimson glare. Careless now of a possible bullet from inside the house, Flint raced across the courtyard. The compulsion for killing was riding him hard, the blood throbbing and pounding through his veins, his whole body afire with the power he experienced. As he reached the corner of the house, a side door opened, spilling a shaft of yellow lamplight into the dimness. Two men stumbled out. One of them was an old, grey-bearded man holding an old-fashioned Peacemaker in his right hand. The light fell squarely on his face as he turned, made to run in Flint's direction, skidded to a halt as he saw the gunman standing there, grinning broadly.

'Macey!' he yelled and fired in the same moment. Flint

had seen the gun lifting, flung himself flat against the wall, heard the thin mosquito whine of the bullet through the tremendous blast of the explosion. He brought up his own gun then, sent a bullet smashing into the oldster's chest, the impact slamming the man back through the doorway through which smoke was already beginning to pour as the roof caught.

The second man uttered a savage roar of anger. He swung his gun on Macey, pulled the trigger. There was a sharp click as the hammer fell on a spent cartridge. Flint curled his lips back over his teeth, walked forward slowly, relishing each moment.

'I guess you're Credin,' he said thinly. 'Seems you were aimin' to throw in your lot with Condor and the others. Foran figured it about time you learned a lesson.' For a moment, he debated whether to shoot the other down in cold blood or not. The urge to do so was strong in him, his finger tightening convulsively on the trigger. Then Clay's hoarse voice yelled from somewhere at the front of the building: 'They're all surrenderin', Flint. They've had enough.'

Slowly, Flint eased the pressure on the trigger, made a quick jerky motion with the gun. 'Get along there with the rest of 'em,' he snarled. 'We're goin' to burn this place to ashes. I figure you can make it back into Benton with anybody who's still alive. Maybe when they hear about this, they'll think twice about goin' against Foran. Now move.'

The Lazy L riders who were still alive were herded into the courtyard, together with Credin's wife who was sobbing hysterically. Their faces were grey and drawn in the flickering glow of the fire which had now spread rapidly until everything was alight. Flint Macey moved over to where Credin stood a little apart from the others, watching all he had fought and lived for go up in flame and smoke. The other turned sharply, his face tight. 'You goddamn stinkin' killer, Macey!' he spat. 'One of these days you're goin' to pay in full for this. Believe me, I'll see you and the rest of these gunhawks swinging from that cottonwood in Benton and—'

'Cut the gab, Credin,' Macey said softly, dangerously softly. He lashed out with the barrel of the Colt, the foresight drawing a long streak of blood down the other man's cheek. 'Be thankful that we haven't shot you and your wife.'

'I'm not afraid of men like you, Macey,' retorted the other. He put up a hand to his bleeding face, eyes narrowed down. 'But I don't intend to place my wife in any further jeopardy.'

There was a fraught silence. For a moment it seemed that Macey would blast away in spite of the fact that the other was unarmed, but some spark of decency remained, staying his hand. 'Now you're seein' sense,' he muttered. Pointing to the far side of the courtyard, well away from the blazing inferno he said: 'There's a buckboard yonder. Hitch a couple of horses to it and get out of here before we change our minds.'

A blazing piece of timber fell from the roof, striking the ground only a few feet away and he yelled over his shoulder, 'Get away from the buildings. They're goin' to cave in at any moment.'

The men scattered as more burning debris fell. By now the barn and bunkhouse were virtually gutted and even as they watched, the walls collapsed inward, jetting sparks high into the air.

Frank Condor was in the small diner when a ranny from the grain store came into the room, looked about him anxiously for a moment, then hastened over to the table at the far side of the room, halting in front of Frank. The other glanced up from his food, chewed thoughtfully on a strip of bacon for a moment, then said softly, 'Lookin' for me?'

'That's right, Marshal. Thought you'd like to know that Frisco is in town. He's over at the saloon right now, braggin' it around that he aims to kill you if you've got the guts to step over there.'

Frank nodded, went back to his meal. It was almost as if he hadn't heard what the other had said. The man paused for a moment, nervously twisting his fingers together, then coughed, said: 'Want me to tell him anythin' Marshal?'

Frank emptied his coffee cup, wiped his mouth with the back of his hand. 'Sure. Tell him I'll be along to accommodate him in a few minutes. Reckon he can have another little while to stay alive.' There was something in the quiet, level tones that sent a little shiver through the other. For a second, he stared down at the marshal, then turned sharply on his heel and hurried out.

Frank ordered another cup of coffee, spooned sugar into it from the china bowl, drank it slowly. He was on the point of rising when someone else came into the room and glancing up sharply, he felt a moment's surprise to see Atalanta Carson standing there. She came over to him, her face concerned.

'You know that Frisco has just ridden in.' She eyed him out of grave, grey eyes. 'I saw his horse tethered outside the saloon.'

'I know,' he nodded, setting down the coffee cup. 'I've just had word that he wants to meet me.'

She saw his lips stretch very thin and tight as he got to his feet, hitched the gunbelt up around his waist. 'You're not going over there?' There was a note of alarm in her voice.

'I have to go,' he replied firmly. 'This is somethin' between him and me, Atalanta.' His voice took on a faintly rough edge. 'I want you to stay here, where you'll be safe. There may be some other Double Circle riders in town and if lead starts to fly, innocent people are likely to get in the way.'

She wanted to say something more, to try to dissauade him from going, but the look of grim determination on his face was one which, she knew, would brook no argument, so she merely sighed, made a futile little gesture with her right hand and stood on one side as he made for the door.

Outside in the street, Frank walked slowly along the dead centre of the road, his eyes seeming to see nothing, yet taking in everything with an unfocused glance. He walked with that unique look of grim confidence which seemed to set him apart from other men. He could sense that there were eyes on him as he walked past, observing him, maybe, knowing where he was headed, and why, but he gave no indication that he saw the onlookers. Glancing neither to right or left, he walked straight for the Fast Gun saloon, paused for a few moments, listening to the faint hum of conversation which came from inside, the occasional burst of raucous laughter.

The exterior of the saloon consisted of the usual eight-foot high façade supported by four strong ironwood poles, a narrow veranda running all the way around the edge of the flat roof. The batwing doors were situated dead centre of the front of the building, with windows set on either side. As Frank paused, he noticed that there were faces pressed close to the panes of the windows, watching his every move, guessed that Frisco had posted a few of the men inside to watch for his coming. Maybe the other was not quite as confident as he had tried to sound.

One of the faces suddenly withdrew. Inside the saloon, Clifford, a tall, sparse man with thin, greying hair, called over his shoulder. 'Here he comes now.' He moved away from the window as he spoke, back into the corner of the room where he figured he would be out of the line of fire if it came to gunplay.

At the bar, Frisco tilted his hat back a little further on his head, but did not turn, content to watch the reflection of the door in the wide mirror along the back of the bar. The batwing doors swung open slowly, letting in a shaft of sunlight. Frank stood framed in the opening for a moment, holding one door in each hand. Then he let them go and stepped inside, the doors creaking shut at his back. He looked about him for a moment, then moved in slow, casual steps towards the bar.

The barkeep, his face pasty and grey, threw a quick, speculative glance at Frisco, standing a few yards away, then sidled over in Frank's direction.

'What'll it be, Marshal?'

'Make it whiskey,' Frank said quietly. 'I'm on duty.'

A man at one of the tables suddenly rose to his feet and moved away to the side of the room. Frank poured himself a drink from the bottle which the barkeep slid across to him, tossed it down in a single gulp.

'I see you're still totin' that badge around on your shirt, Condor,' said Frisco softly. He spoke from ten feet along the bar without turning his head.

'Reckon if you're to get a bullet, it had better be done legal,' Frank said. He saw the abrupt stiffening of the other's shoulders, saw the killer's face change, his eyes clamping down into slits, his lips pursed. Then he forced himself to relax as though recognizing that Frank was deliberately trying to rile him, force him into action before he was good and ready.

Frisco smiled. He shrugged his shoulders, still standing with his elbows hard on the bar. He held his glass between both hands. 'You talk big, Marshal. Reckon you're forgettin' that you're a little out of practice with those guns of yours. You may have been fast a couple of years ago, down in Texas, but you haven't handled 'em since then. That's sure goin' to cost you your life.'

'Seems to me you're all set to kill me by talkin'.'

For a moment there was no sound whatever in the saloon. Outside, a horse snickered near the tethering rail and in the distance, a dog howled thinly, the weird cry wailing on the breeze that stirred the dust in the street.

Frisco turned slowly to face Frank. His narrow, uncompromising mouth was drawn out, flattened down. He shifted his weight slightly, spread both legs a little, now standing clear of the bar to give plenty of room to his gun arm.

'You've just talked yourself into your own grave, Condor,' he said ominously. 'You're not buskin' any of the Double Circle riders now.'

Frank set down his glass, turned slowly. There was the promise of death in his eyes as he faced the gunhawk. 'If you reckon I've slowed with the gun, then this is your chance to find out, Frisco,' he murmured. He was watching the other's eyes and mouth, looking for the faint change that would come over the other's face in the split second before he made his play. 'We've put up with your kind in Benton too long now and—'

'Condor!' It was the barkeep who uttered the single word of warning. Somehow, Frisco had felt his killer's courage ebbing away from him as he had faced up to Condor. He had never come up against a gunman like this before and he no longer felt so certain that he was faster than the man who faced him. Deciding that he needed an edge to make sure of killing Frank, he had diverted the other's attention long enough to get it. His hand moved down with a blur of speed, taloned fingers clawing for the gunbutt in his belt. The gun was about two-thirds clear of the leather when there came a deafening explosion, a glare of blue-crimson from somewhere in front of him and the smashing impact of lead, driving deep within his chest, thrust him hard back against the bar. For a long moment he hung there, his right hand dropping, the gun barrel tilted downward at the floor. Then, his knees seemed to spring outward as if they had been kicked from behind and he jack-knifed backward, his head hitting the top of the counter with a sickening thud. The gun fell from his fingers and clattered to the wooden floor beside him.

The barkeep had seen nothing of Frank's draw. All he had seen was the sudden eruption of black powder-smoke and the faint crimson lash of gunflame from the long barrel of the Colt. Now he leaned forward, peering over the top of the bar, eyes popping from his head as he stared at the body lying just below him.

Slowly, a look of stupefied astonishment written all over his fleshy features, he looked up, said in a faintly choking tone: 'Somebody better go for Doc Fortune.'

'Won't be no need for that,' Frank said confidently, scarcely looking at the dead killer as he pouched the gun. 'He's dead, Better get the undertaker.'

Moving back to the bar, he tilted the whiskey bottle with a steady hand, refilling his glass. Outside in the street, he heard the commotion as the echoes of that single shot rattled among the buildings. There came the sound of running feet on the boardwalk outside and a moment later, Talbot came in, his gun drawn. He looked stupidly at the figure sprawled near the bar, then put the gun away.

'Hell,' he breathed. 'I'd never have believed it if I hadn't seen it with my own eyes. This is sure goin' to rock Foran back on his heels.'

Frank nodded, glanced at the sheriff over the rim of his glass, pushed the bottle towards him. 'Maybe so. But while he still has the Macey brothers on his payroll, he won't back off. He's risked everythin' now. He can't go back on what he set out to do.'

Talbot grunted. 'This ought to make the other ranchers sit up, though. With Frisco dead, it means the end of Foran's right-hand gun. He relied on him to back up his play.'

Two men came into the saloon, went over to the body, lifted it unceremoniously and carried it out, the doors swinging shut behind them. Frank finished his drink, then excused himself, went out into the street. As he stepped down from the boardwalk, he could make out Atalanta Carson standing on the far side, a hundred yards away. She ran towards him as he walked towards her. 'Is he—?'

'Frisco's dead,' he told her soberly. 'But knowing Foran, it won't stop him from going ahead with his plans. He still has more than forty men, and the Maceys are still with him.'

'I want you to ride back with me, Frank,' she said suddenly. 'That's why I rode into town. One or two of the other ranchers gave Dad their promise to come over tonight with their men. He's planning to ride against the Double Circle spread. I know that nothing I can say will make him change his mind and maybe it's the only thing for him to do, but I'd feel easier in my mind if I knew you were riding with him.'

Frank nodded. 'I'll come,' he said simply. 'With Frisco dead, I doubt it there'll be any more trouble here in town. Besides, I think that one or two of the townsfolk have already decided that there's got to be a change around here. Foran has been havin' it all his own way for too long now. They've just woken up to the fact that this is their town and it's up to them to say how it's to be run.'

'I've got the buckboard waiting.' She held his arm as they walked together along the boardwalk, the loud echoes of their footsteps preceding them. As they drew level with the sheriff's office, Talbot came hurrying across from the direction of the saloon. He looked from the girl to Frank, then back again with a faint expression of puzzlement on his face.

'Atalanta came to tell me that some of the others are joinin' Phil at his place tonight. They're gettin' ready to move against Foran. I figure I should ride with 'em.'

'You want me to come along?' Talbot asked. 'I could possibly round up a handful of men from town. After that exhibition of gunplay in the saloon there I figure there are a few who'll throw in their lot with us.'

Frank shook his head. 'Better keep them here in town just in case Foran should manage to slip past us and try to get Carron out of jail again.'

'I'll do that,' Talbot promised. He climbed up on to the plankwalk as Frank helped the girl into the buckboard, then got up beside her, taking up the reins.

The sun was already low, weltering towards the distant hills as they rode out of town, keeping to the main valley trail. Ahead of them, the hills were silent against the heavens and far to the north, the tall peaks of the mountains were touched with a pale crimson, glowing with splashes of colour that blended with the deep-shadowed green of the pines on the lower slopes. Off to the south, the Red glittered in the late afternoon sunlight and – fifteen minutes later – they clattered over a long plank bridge which had been thrown over the river.

This was a wonderful country, Frank thought musingly. The pity was that men with the habits of wolves, men such as Foran and the Maceys, had to move in and spoil it. He thought of the coming night with a faint dampening of his spirits. A lot of good men were going to die just to make this territory safe for decent men and women to live in.

'You're very quiet,' Atalanta said, after the silence had grown between them. 'Somethin' on your mind?' She was watching him in the same manner as he had noticed earlier, out of extremely grave eyes.

'I'm thinkin' of Foran and how we can fight him without too many men gettin' themselves killed,' he told her soberly. 'I guess I've lived with violence for too long, I can't help thinkin' this way.'

Atalanta pursed her lips. 'I think I can understand how you feel, Frank. I was only a little girl when we came here. My mother died shortly after we arrived in Benton. It was hard in those days, fighting the outlaws, even the Indians, and there were always the bad years when the rains never came and the crops failed. But we managed to survive and for a while it seemed that we had beaten most things, that there would be nothing else to trouble us. Then Foran came along and it all started up again.' She sighed softly, leaned against him. 'I often wonder if there will ever be an end to it.'

'An end to what?' he asked quietly.

'To all of this shooting and burning and killing. Why do men have to act like animals?'

'I guess it's a law of nature,' he replied. He felt a little out of his depth at the turn of the conversation. 'There are always some men who want a little more than what they've got. They covet their neighbour's land and cattle and when they can't get them by fair means, they resort to the gun. It may be that one day, there'll be peace here, but I don't know when.'

'Surely this territory is big enough for everybody to get as much as he needs?'

'There are always some who want more than they need. I've seen them come and I've seen them go. Most of them end up in Boot Hill with only six feet of earth to their name.'

The girl shivered as if a cold breeze had touched her, although the air was uncomfortably warm. She fell silent, engrossed in her own private thoughts as Frank brought the reins down hard on the rumps of the horses, urging them forward at a faster gait. The country around them now was flatter than before. They had left the rolling hills behind and less than five miles away lay the lush grass which marked the perimeter of her father's spread.

6

Night of the Long Shadows

There were a few motionless silhouettes of men standing in the shadows around the ranch house as they drove down the hill trail into the courtyard. Elsewhere, judging by the look of activity that was going on around the place, it was evident that Phil Carson had meant every word he had said about attacking Foran. Frank noticed there were plenty of new horses in the corral, indicating that some of the ranchers had responded to the call to join together to fight the Circle boys. He stretched his stiff legs as he climbed down from the buckboard, turned as Phil Carson came out of the shadows.

'I'll see that you get a horse if you're joinin' us, Frank,' he said calmly. He stretched out an arm to embrace the scene. 'We're gettin' ready to finish this chore. We've stood by long enough, watchin' Foran ride in and grab all he wants. Reckon you can push men so far, but no further.'

'Atalanta has told me what you intend to do,' Frank nodded. 'Could be though that this is what Foran is wantin' you to do, ride in to him so he can pick his own ground.'

Carson drew heavily on his cigarette, then dropped the

glowing butt and ground it into the dirt with his heel. 'I've thought about that, Frank. Maybe there is some truth in it, but we'll gain nothin' by waiting for him to come to us. All the time, he's growin' stronger, bringing in killers like the Maceys from as far away as Texas, payin' them blood money to kill innocent men and women, while we're simply standin' still. If you've got some other plan, I'm mighty willin' to hear it though.'

'No, I've no other plan. One thing in our favour though. Frisco's dead.'

Carson's face mirrored his surprise. 'Frisco dead,' he repeated. 'You sure about that? How'd it happen?'

'He called me out in the saloon in Benton,' Frank replied calmly. 'He maybe figured he was faster than he really was.'

'Hell,' breathed the other. He whistled thinly through his teeth. 'I wonder if Foran knows.'

'I guess that Foran sent him into town in order to kill me. Frisco had no personal quarrel with me. He was just a gunslinger ready to kill anyone, so long as the price was right.'

'And the Maceys?'

'They're no doubt still around. They'll back Foran to the hilt.'

'How can you be so sure of that? If they suddenly discover that they're on the losin' side, they'll pull out faster'n a bronc with a rattler on his tail.'

Frank shook his head. 'I don't think they will. You see, they've both got a personal score to settle with me. I reckon they'll stick around even if Foran pays 'em nothin'.'

'So it's like that.' Carson gave a brief nod. Turning, he led the way into the house. 'Better get a bite to eat before we ride out. It's goin' to be a mighty long night for all of us.'

With the meal soon over, Frank made his way out into

the yard again. There were several men there now, tightening the cinches under their horses' bellies, or checking their rifles. Frank recognized men from some of the other outfits, reckoned there were perhaps thirty-five men or so riding with them. At least they would meet Foran's gun crew on virtually equal terms. Whether that would be enough, he was not sure. These men were not professional killers as Foran's men were and he was uncertain how the majority of them might react when the shooting started. Still, it was the only course open to them and if they managed to get the advantage of surprise on their side, it might swing the fight in their favour.

'Anybody else likely to come in?' he asked as Carson came over.

The other looked about him, eyes peering into the growing darkness that lay like a deep sable pall over the countryside. 'Don't see Credin and any of his boys around,' he said eventually. 'I'd have figured they'd sure be along.'

'Maybe he's on his way,' Frank nodded. 'I got the feelin' he was a little reluctant to throw in with any attack on Foran at the meeting we had in Benton. But I'd have figured things had changed a little since then, with Carron still locked away in jail in spite of everythin' Foran has been able to do to bust him out.'

Carson opened his mouth to say something, but at that moment one of the men called sharply. 'Buckboard headin' this way, fast. Just comin' over the hill yonder.'

Frank stared off into the deepening darkness where the faint glimmering of starlight showed the rise of the hill, picking out the silhouette of the buckboard. A few moments later, Frank was able to make out the handful of men who rode close behind it.

'Looks like Credin,' he said, puzzled. 'Why didn't he bring all of his men with him?'

'There's somethin' wrong.' Phil Carson started forward as the buckboard neared the courtyard.

Frank was close behind him as the small party stopped. He felt a distinct shock of stunned surprise as he let his gaze wander over the tiny group, from Credin, sitting forward behind the reins, his face smoke-blackened, so that only his eyes seemed alive in a black mask, his wife leaning back on the wooden seat, face streaked with tears and the silent, chastened men who rode slowly behind.

'Good God, man!' muttered Carson. 'What happened?' He extended a hand to help Mrs Carson out of the wagon.

Letting the reins fall, Credin said in a low terrible voice: 'Some of Foran's men hit us a little while ago. They killed more than half of my crew, fired all of the buildings. There's nothing left now.' He paused brokenly as his wife began to weep hysterically in great, racking sobs that threatened to tear her frail frame apart.

Atalanta came out of the house, took her by the arm. 'I'll take care of her, Dad,' she said. She helped the woman into the ranch.

'This is bad news,' Carson said solemnly. 'We were figuring on ridin' out to Foran's spread and finishing this once and for all. Most of the others are in it with us. We were waiting for you to accompany us but—'

Credin drew himself up to his full height. His face was terrible to see. 'We'll ride with you, Phil,' he said in a hoarse tone. 'I've got nothin' left to live for now. Those killers destroyed everythin'. Maybe if I'd been wise and listened to the marshal here things could have been different. I've paid for my own folly. But I'll die happy if I can take some more of those critters with me before I die.'

'Are you sure you can make it?' Carson asked concernedly.

'Don't worry none about us,' growled the other. 'Me and the boys did some hard talkin' on the way here. They're all in this with me.'

'Did you see how many men were in the force that attacked you, Credin?' Frank asked tautly.

'Hard to say. They hit us without warnin' and there was so much shootin' going on around the house. Then they tossed in firebrands and that finished it. We never had a chance.'

'Reckon there was about a dozen of 'em all together. Marshal,' put in one of the other men. 'I don't figure there were many more than that. The Macey brothers were with 'em.'

'So that means that Foran's forces are split. If we can hit him before that other bunch get back, we stand a far better chance.'

'Then what are we waitin' for?' called Carson loudly. He shouted up the rest of the men, waited while they swung up into the saddle, then mounted up himself. 'Let's go!'

They rode out in a wide bunch, leaving behind the slow-settling streamers of grey dust. They stayed with the main trail upward for half a mile and then swung off it into a series of small undulating meadows which criss-crossed the hills that creased the heavy folds of ground bordering on the desert. Soon they were in the heavy timber and the starlight was shut out so that they seemed to be riding in a great muffling well of silence, the thick carpet of deadfall drowning the sound of their passing. The timber, Frank noticed, was first-growth pine, tall trunks, massive at the butt, tapering up for almost thirty feet before the out-spreading branches and leaves formed a solid ceiling over their heads. There was little underbrush here and they were able to make good progress. In the lead, Carson set a steady course to the west with the dim shapes of the tall trees running before them on all sides. By degrees, the terrain roughened. They splashed across several narrow, but fast-running, streams that raced in white foamed torrents down the hillside from their sources high among the ridges. They held to the crests of the humped ridges for as long as possible, then dropped down into the rough-floored ravines, crossed over, rode up a steep slope where the canyon walls crowded in so closely on both sides that two men were unable to ride abreast and the sharp edged rocks caught at their legs and scraped their horses' flanks.

Near two o'clock in the morning, with the moon just beginning to show on the eastern horizon, the trees gave way and they faced a wide creek running noisily over its smooth stones.

Staying within shelter, Carson edged his mount forward into the open a little way, scanned the stillness which lay spread out before him, watching the upper and lower reaches of the valley below until he was finally satisfied. Far off, there was a starved echo, swiftly dying into silence. He lifted himself a little in the saddle, listening for it to be repeated and when it was not, he waved a hand to the others.

'There's Foran's spread,' he said as Frank drew level with him. 'My guess is that he may have look-outs posted. If he has, we may lose the advantage of surprise.'

'Want me to scout ahead?' Frank asked.

'I'd sure feel easier in my mind if you did. I don't relish invitin' a bullet out of the shadows.'

Frank nodded, gigged his mount forward, eyes roving ahead of him. He stayed within shelter, came to where a trail looped downward off the switchback courses and since there was no other way down, he took it.

The Double Circle look-out had shown no ingenuity in his choice of position. Frank spotted the tall upthrusting column of rock while he was still some distance away. It stood out from the flat ground, solitary and unmistakable, touched with moonlight, clearly commanding such a dominating position that it was the only possible place for a man to bide his time if he had orders to watch the trail. Silently, Frank slid from the saddle, drifted into the under-growth which grew thickly at this point along the trail. He could see nothing of any man watching the trail, but he was taking no chances and less than three minutes later, the faint snicker of a horse from up ahead reached his ears.

Picking his way forward cautiously, he circled the rocky outcrop, eased his long body carefully over the patches of open ground, his gaze probing the long, moon-thrown shadows which lay around the rocks. A few moments later, he spotted the horse tethered to a storm-splintered stump and lifting his gaze he picked out the prone figure of a man lying on a flat ledge of stone, a rifle propped up beside him.

It was clear from the man's attitude that he had no inkling of his danger. Even as Frank watched him, the man twisted his body, dug into his shirt pocket and brought out the makings of a smoke, propping himself up on one elbow to roll the long strands of tobacco in the brown paper. Frank had no strong desire to shoot the other down in cold blood and there was also the distinct possibility that a gunshot would carry some distance on a clear night such as this, probably warn Foran of trouble. There was only one thing for it. He would have to get sufficiently close to take the other by surprise before he could get his hands on that nearby rifle.

The intervening stretch of ground was open; bare rock with scarcely any cover. He waited a full two minutes while the look-out got his cigarette going, then moved snake-like over the hard ground, head low, praying that the other man would not turn his head, but the other seemed intent on watching the trail that led away to his left. Obviously not an imaginative man, he did not even consider the possibility of anyone creeping up on him from the rear.

Frank was within ten feet of him before some inner instinct seemed to warn the other of danger. The man jerked his head around abruptly, peering into the dimness behind him. Before he could utter a single sound, Frank got his legs under him, thrust himself off the ground, his head butting the man in the midriff before he could rise.

The other's clawing fingers jerked out for the rifle, managed to rake across the butt. The breath escaped from his lips in an explosive whoosh as he fell back, head hitting the solid rock with a stunning force.

Realizing that the rifle was now out of his reach, the man clawed for his sixgun, had it half drawn from the holster when the descending gunbutt in Frank's hand connected with a sickening crunch on his right temple. He was unconscious before his body hit the ground. Breathing hard, Frank got to his feet, took the other's rifle and guns, tossed them into the rocks, then clambered down on to the trail, made his way back to where his mount stood waiting patiently and rode back to join the others.

'All clear?' asked Carson.

Frank nodded. 'They had a man on watch along the trail a piece. He won't bother us now.'

All of the horses stirred again as Carson gave the signal to move ahead. Frank bent forward in the saddle and stared straight ahead of him, watching details appear out of the dimness. As yet, the moon had not risen sufficiently to throw enough light over the terrain to see things clearly and they were almost on top of the Double Circle ranch before they were aware of it. Lights glowed yellowly in the windows and from where they had drawn rein, they could just make out the shapes of men in the courtyard, between the ranch house and the bunkhouse some fifty yards distant.

'Looks like we ain't expected,' grunted Credin tautly. He drew the long-barrelled Winchester from its scabbard, levered it softly. His face was twisted into a scowl of pure hatred. Frank could guess at the thoughts that were running through the other's mind at that moment and could feel sympathy with him, yet there was a vague sense of warning in his brain as he watched the rancher slide from the saddle. A man filled with such a bitter hatred as

Credin was unlikely to think clearly when it came to a gun battle and that could be both dangerous and perhaps fatal.

'Take it easy, friend,' he said softly. 'You'll get your chance at Foran before long.'

With an effort, the other relaxed and a little of the tension seeped out of his body. 'I'll be all right,' he whispered back. 'It's just that I can't forget what happened back there when those devils attacked us.'

'Everybody spread out,' said Carson, coming forward. 'Nobody open fire until they hear my signal, two shots in quick succession.'

The men slipped away into the darkness, circling the cluster of buildings. Frank and Credin put down a small wrinkle in the ground, crouched down in a tiny hollow from where they could watch the front door that led directly on to the porch. A chill breath of night air swept over them as they waited. Frank could feel the other shivering convulsively, but whether from the cold of the night or from suppressed tension, he could not tell. In the dimness, he felt all of the chambers in his guns, ensured that they were all loaded. Then he fell to watching the house.

A man stepped out on to the porch, closing the door quickly behind him. He had a smoke in his hand and the tiny red glow winked on and off as he drew on the cigarette, leaning his shoulders against one of the uprights. Another pair of men drifted out of the bunkhouse, were on their way towards the corral when the twin shots blasted out from a little way over on Frank's left.

Scarcely had the echoes died away than a thunderous volley of gunfire open up. The two men in the yard crumpled, falling to their knees without a chance to draw their guns. The man on the porch, whom Frank took to be Witney Foran, although at that distance it was impossible to be certain of his identity, ducked swiftly out of sight, crawling behind the rain barrel at the end of the porch where it afforded him a little protection from the flying lead.

Above the din of gunfire, Carson's voice called out. 'Now you're gettin' a taste of your own medicine, Foran. This is the end of the line as far as you're concerned.'

There was no answer from the ranch. Over near the corral, two men suddenly broke cover, ducked beneath the rails and ran for the horses – which were milling nervously on the far side. The distance was too far for hand guns and both men succeeded in swinging up on to their mount's backs, clinging precariously to them without any saddles for support. Frank had to feel a sense of grudging admiration for the way both men handled their mounts, putting them to the fence, leaping into the courtyard, setting them towards the trail that wound up from the ranch.

'Get those two men!' called Carson harshly.

Guns roared spitefully as the men thundered past. One of the riders suddenly released his hold on his mount's neck, reared up in the saddle, arms thrown high over his head. He toppled sideways, hit the ground hard and rolled over several times before coming to rest at the bottom of the slope. In the moonlight, his wide open eyes stared sightlessly at the star-strewn heavens.

His companion almost made it before a bullet nicked his horse's neck. The animal shied with a shrill whinny of pain, unseating him. He crashed into the brush, lay still for a moment, then lunged forward, diving for cover behind a fallen tree. The riderless horse plunged on over the brow of the hill, the tattoo of its hooves fading swiftly into the distance.

'Stay here,' Frank whispered urgently to Credin. 'I'm goin' after that *hombre* down there.' He wriggled off through the tall grass. A bullet cut through the air within an inch of his head and out of the corner of his eye, he caught sight of the brief lance of crimson flame that spouted from the gunman's Colt. Now that he had the other pinpointed. Frank glanced around at the surrounding terrain. It would be impossible for the man to move back without exposing himself; on the other hand, he commanded a view of the open ground on every side of him. Drawing up his legs, he arched his back, dug in his heels and palmed his Colt. Breathing deeply for the space of perhaps ten seconds, he sprinted forward as fast as the thrust of his legs would carry him.

Immediately, a second gunshot blasted and there came another lancing tongue of scarlet flame. The breath of the passing bullet touched his cheek and he threw himself bodily to the ground, twisting instinctively as he landed. There was gunfire all about him now, but as far as he was concerned, there was only this one man who mattered. Snapping off a quick shot as he hit the dirt, he saw a broad dagger of wood slice off the dead tree and fly into the air.

Before the other could lift his head and sight his gun again, Frank loosed off three rapid shots, placing them in a pattern around the deadfall. Then he flattened himself to the ground once more, drawing the other gun and thrusting the empty weapon back into its holster. He was so close that he could hear the man's harsh breathing although he could not see him. A ricochet from somewhere in the darkness, whipped along his arm, burning the flesh without actually penetrating, alerting him to the danger that lay all about him now that he had deliberately exposed himself to a marksman inside the ranch.

Seconds dragged by on leaden feet as he lay quite still, the Colt resting on his out-thrust arm, sighted so that he could move it swiftly to pick any spot along the top of the tree trunk. Lancing fingers of cramp seared through the muscles of his thighs, knotting them painfully. The urge to straighten his legs, to ease the agony, was almost more than he could fight down.

Then, when he had begun to despair of the other making any move, he saw the crown of a hat appear near the end of the trunk. He swung the gun instinctively, was on the point of squeezing the trigger when he noticed the way in which the hat wobbled. Drawing his lips back across his teeth, he held his fire. It was an old trick, but it had almost worked. The other was lifting his hat on the end of a stick, hoping to draw his fire and give away his exact position. He realized now that he was lying in a small hollow, not deep enough to shelter him, but sufficiently so for a long shadow to be lying across his body making it difficult for the other to pick him out against the background of grass and rock.

After a few moments, the hat vanished, withdrawn quickly. Again, Frank forced himself to wait. Then he heard the sharp intake of breath which gave the other away. There was the scrape of booted heels on rock and without warning, the gunhawk launched himself sideways, diving for the bushes to one side. The move almost took Frank by surprise. He fired instinctively, without pausing to take deliberate aim, heard the first slug strike wood. The second, however, thudded into yielding flesh and the man fell awkwardly, a branch snapping loudly under his weight. Before he could move into cover, the barrel of Frank's Colt tipped downward and the man fell back with a bullet in his chest.

By the time he had worked his way back to where Credin lay, pumping shot after shot into the ranch house, the fire from the barn and bunkhouse had noticeably slackened. Caught on the wrong foot, many of the Double Circle crew had been in the open when the attack had begun, had been shot down before they could reach cover. Narrowing his eyes, Frank searched for some sign of the dark figure he had noticed on the porch. but could see no indication of any movement. Either the other was dead, or he was keeping himself well concealed.

There was still plenty of return fire from the rear of the ranch house, however, and it was obvious to Frank that the defenders were in a pretty strong position, unless they could rush the place. Before this could be done, however, a further danger presented itself.

Two men came down out of the trees in a hurry, their feet crashing through the tangled underbrush. Frank glanced round swiftly, jerking up his gun, then lowered it as he recognized two of Credin's men.

'A bunch of men headin' this way,' said one of them breathlessly. 'Could be the Maceys with the rest of the Double Circle outfit, those who attacked us earlier tonight.'

'If it is, then they'll have heard the gunfire by now and know there's trouble.' Frank spoke incisively. 'We've got to stop them before they manage to break through and join up with Foran down there.'

'How do you figure on doin' that?' queried Credin.

'We'll make our stand among the trees yonder. From there we can cover the trail over the hill. They may not be expectin' that.'

'I'll come with you. Forbes and Withers, get two more men. Hurry!'

They made for a small, flinty knoll set among the trees and settled down to wait, the faint drumming of hooves clearly audible now, even above the continued roar of gunfire at their backs. After a few moments, Frank was able to make out the bunch of riders in the moonlight, spurring their mounts forward at a cruel pace. There was no doubt whatever in his mind now that it was Flint and Clay Macey, returning after their nocturnal mission to burn out Credin and his family.

As a sudden thought passed through his mind he turned sharply to the rancher lying prone beside him. 'Don't open fire until I give the word,' he hissed urgently. 'I want them as close as possible before they know we're here. With a little luck we can empty half of those saddles before they're aware of us.'

Credin tightened his lips, then nodded tersely. It was clear that the order settled hard with him, but he was forced to admit the wisdom of such strategy.

The heavy party ran full tilt up the narrow trail and as they came on, two abreast, Frank recognized the Macey brothers in the lead. They were perhaps a hundred feet away when someone in the party yelled: 'Hole up, Flint. We're liable to run into trouble if we barge in there with our eyes shut. They could have somebody watchin' their rear.'

The column slackened speed at the shout. Frank thrust his body down in the undergrowth, thus to become absorbed in the black shadow of it. He heard Flint Macey call: 'Dismount and spread out.'

Frank sighted along his gun. This was to be the last chance they would get before the men went down under cover and scattered. 'Open fire,' he yelled harshly.

Gunfire ripped the night into a thousand screaming fragments of sound. Four men tumbled from their saddles before they had a chance to obey Macey's orders. The others fought to check their rearing mounts, then galloped into the thick brush as more bullets followed them. Frank estimated that both of the Maceys had survived that initial fusillade and there could only be five or six men still alive.

At least they had reduced the odds nearer to evens. Lifting his head cautiously, he watched for any movement that would give away the position of any of the gunmen. For a long moment, there was nothing. Then a black shadow broke away from the massed shadows beneath the trees, raced for the cover of a thick bush ten yards away. Frank snapped a shot at the man, missed and cursed harshly under his breath. 'You don't have a chance, any of you,' he called loudly, raising his voice to make himself heard above the booming racket of gunfire nearer the Double Circle ranch. 'Foran is finished. Throw out your guns and come out with your hands lifted.'

'Go to hell, Condor.' Clay Macey's voice came from among the trees. 'I'm goin' to have the pleasure of seein' you die, real slow.'

'The last time you see me, you'll be danglin' from a branch,' Frank called back. He sent a couple of shots probing into the brush, but the other must have shifted his position the moment he had finished speaking. Sporadic firing continued as they forced the Double Circle men to keep their heads down; and behind them, Frank was aware that the gunfire around the ranch house was dying slowly.

Ten minutes later, it had died out altogether. From a few feet away, Credin murmured: 'Reckon it's all over back there, one way or the other.'

Frank nodded. The silence from the valley was suddenly ominous. Then Phil Carson's voice drifted up from down the slope. 'Witney Foran's dead. It's all over.'

'You hear that?' Frank shouted. 'Your boss is dead. If you want to go on shootin' that's all right by us. If you want to give up, step out now with your hands high.'

He waited, the hammer of his Colt thumbed back. For a moment there was silence. Then he heard a faint movement in the brush and a second later, three men stepped out, their hands high.

'They're surrenderin',' said Credin tautly. He made to get to his feet, but Frank pulled him down.

'Where's Flint and Clay Macey?' he called sharply. He let his glance slide sideways towards the midnight shadows that lay thick and huge among the trees, eyes alert and watchful for trickery. 'Where the hell are they?'

'They—' began one of the men. Before he could go on, the sound of horses moving swiftly down-grade reached Frank's ears. With a muttered oath, he leapt to his feet, ran forward, thrust the three men aside in his run.

Reaching the edge of the trees he stared out into the moonlight, was just in time to see the two riders spurring their mounts down towards the distant valley. Thrusting the Colt back into leather, he turned away. The others had too much of a lead for him to hope to catch them.

'Where'd you figure they'll head for?' Carson asked, when Frank told him, a little while later, after the last of the surviving Double Circle riders had been rounded up.

'If they've any sense, they'll ride on over the hill and keep on riding,' he said soberly. 'But I've got that feelin' in my bones, they won't.'

'Ain't nothin' left for them to do around here. Foran's no longer around to pay 'em.'

Frank clenched his teeth until the muscles of his jaw lumped painfully. 'They didn't come here just because Foran sent for 'em and paid 'em to ride for him. They had another reason for wantin' to be around Benton.'

'What kind of reason?'

'They came to kill me. An old score from way back, down in Texas.'

Carson's brows drew together into a straight line as he pondered that. Then he nodded. 'I suppose I guessed that some time ago,' he said simply. He looked about him at the ruin of a once-proud ranch. 'We're finished here. Reckon we'd better be ridin' on back.' He jerked a thumb towards the gunmen. 'Reckon that Sheriff Talbot will be glad to give accommodation to these hellions until we can fix up a trial for 'em.'

It was high noon in Benton, the blistering heat laying a pall of shimmering haze and dust over the town, picking out the peeling paint on the front of the livery stables, showing in all its glaring harshness the ugly lines of the stores and the two-storied hotel. In the shade of the boardwalk, several of the older citizens were trying to find some respite from the heat. For a while, Benton seemed its usual self; then, quite suddenly, things changed.

It was Len Hudson, the clerk at the general store, who saw them first, riding in from the desert, saw them and recognized them and ran along the echo-ringing board-walk to warn Sheriff Talbot.

The other was dozing in his chair, his feet on top of the desk, his hat brim pulled well down over his perspiring face. He pushed it back with a show of irritation as the other burst into the office, breathing shallowly with the heat and the exertion.

'What the hell's wrong with you, boy?' he asked harshly. 'Lord, you look as if you've seen a ghost.'

The other swallowed convulsively, his adam's apple working in his throat for several seconds before he managed to speak, one hand pointing a trembling finger towards the street outside.

'Flint and Clay Macey. I saw 'em both riding into town.'

Talbot leapt from his chair as if he had received a shock, moved quickly around the edge of his desk and gripped the youth's shoulder hard. 'You sure, boy?' he asked tightly. 'You could've been mistaken.'

'I couldn't mistake those two characters,' said the other positively. 'It was the Macey brothers, I tell you.'

'All right. Simmer down. Let's go take a look.' He made his way slowly to the street door, opened it a crack and peered out into the dusty sunlight. The inferno heat of the noon sun struck him with the force of a physical blow. For a moment he stood there, then opened the door wider, stepped out carefully on to the boardwalk as though expecting it to collapse under his weight at any moment. Then he turned his head slowly and squinted up and down the street, before stepping back inside. 'Ain't nobody out there now,' he said, ticked by suspicion. 'Now if this is your idea of a joke, I'll—'

'They were there, Sheriff. I swear it.'

'Then they ain't there no longer.' Talbot thought for a

while, a frown creasing his fleshy features. Then he reached a sudden decision. 'You got any idea where Marshal Condor is right now?'

'Sure. He's over at the hotel talking with Miss Carson.'

'Right. Then hurry over there and tell him what you've just told me. I figure he'll know what to do about it. Try not to be seen.'

The clerk hesitated for a moment, then shrugged, stepped out into the street and ran in the direction of the hotel as fast as his legs would carry him. From the door of the sheriff's office, Talbot watched him go, saw him reach the hotel and rush inside. Rubbing his chin, Talbot went over to the rack and took down one of the Winchesters, went over to his desk, took out a box of shells, broke the seal, then thrust a handful into his pocket, loading the rifle carefully. If the boy had been right, he told himself, then it was possible that Frank would need a little help. He could guess at the way those gunmen's minds worked. They would split up, come into two alleys and work their way towards the centre of town, to take Frank from two directions.

Frank and the girl sat at the table near the window on the lower floor of the hotel. There was little breeze and even here, inside the room, the heat was intolerable. When the door opened and the store clerk rushed in, Frank felt a sudden twinge of apprehension. There was something in the other's manner which spoke of trouble.

'Glad I found you here, Marshal.' The other shot a quick glance out of the window. 'I came to warn you that the Macey brothers just rode into town. I saw them from the store. They rode in from the desert. By the time I got to the sheriff's office, they'd split up. Sheriff Talbot says you'll know what to do about it.' He cocked his head on one side and stared at Frank hopefully.

Frank heard Atalanta's sudden intake of breath, could guess at the thoughts which had prompted it. He turned to face her, held her by the arms and looked into her troubled face.

'I have to go,' he said simply. 'You know why they're here.'

'To settle some old score they have with you.' Her voice shook a little. 'Why do you have to go on killing? Is there to be no end to it?'

'This is somethin' between them and me, Atalanta. Something that has to be settled, one way or the other, right here and now. They're out there somewhere, waitin' for me.'

'Don't you mean they're hiding somewhere, ready to bushwhack you the minute you step out of here?'

'Maybe so.' His voice was quite steady. 'Now I want you to stay here until I came back. This won't take long.'

'If you ever come back,' she said, struggling to keep the bitterness out of her voice. 'Those men are cold-blooded killers. They don't go by any of the rules in the book. They'll shoot you in the back and ride out of here laughing.'

'I'll be careful,' he promised.

'Will you, Frank?' The girl's face was fearful.

'I'll make a good try.' He forced a quick smile. 'I'll try real hard.'

Altogether there were perhaps a hundred buildings in Benton, stretching for close on a quarter of a mile on either side of the wide, dusty road. For the most part, they clustered closely together as if for support and this had the effect of narrowing any of the alleys between them, leaving plenty of shadows in which a gunman might hide, ready to pick off his victim without warning. All of this struck Frank forcibly as he walked slowly down the dead centre of the street, his eyes moving swiftly from side to side. It was a damned good town for an ambush and the Maceys were past masters of this sort of thing. They rarely, if ever, faced a man down in fair fight, but relied on taking him by surprise, one of them calling him out in the street while the other sneaked up on him from behind, shooting him in the back without warning.

He was acutely conscious of this possibility as he walked slowly forward, his hands swinging loosely at his sides. There was a tight spot just between his shoulder blades and he found himself hunching forward unconsciously. With an effort he forced himself to relax, telling himself that a shoulder was no good at stopping a bullet, that he made a good enough target for a dry-gulcher.

The town around him seemed utterly deserted. It was so like a ghost town that it was hard to believe there was any other living soul in it apart from himself. Word had obviously travelled fast that the Maceys had ridden in and were looking for vengeance. As he walked, he noticed the two sweat-lathered horses tied up outside one of the stores very near the edge of town, guessed they were those belonging to the Maceys.

There was a narrow alley leading off to his right, its entrance in deep shadow. One of the buildings flanking it was an abandoned grain store, three stories high, with an open door in the topmost floor through which the bags of grain used to be lowered. Frank took all of this in, with a single sweeping glance, putting himself in the Maceys' shoes, wondering what they would do.

He stood absolutely still almost opposite the alley, fingertips less than three inches from the gunbutts in his belt. He stood there for three minutes, was on the point of turning to go back when Flint Macey's voice said loudly:

'Figured you might turn up, Marshal.' He stepped out of the alley into the sunlight. There was an ugly sneer on his face. 'Reckon this is where you collect payment in full for what happened down in Texas.'

'You tried that once before and it didn't come off. What makes you think you can do any better now?' Even as he

spoke, Frank let his gaze move swiftly towards the buildings on either side of him, looking for the slightest tell-tale
movement which would give away Clay Macey's presence,
waiting to pull the same trick these two had worked on so
many occasions in the past. As yet, he could see no sign of
him, but he knew that the other was somewhere close by,
possibly with a Winchester already drawing a bead on his
back, ready to open up the moment he went for his gun.

'Guess we were just a mite unlucky the last time,'
sneered the other. 'But it's goin' to be different now. Any
man can shoot down his brother in cold blood. but when
it comes to stackin' up against seasoned gunmen, you
won't find it so easy.'

Frank felt a savage surge of anger rush through him,
tightening all of the muscles in his body. It was only by a
tremendous effort of will that he kept his composure,
recognizing that the other was trying to rile him. He shook
his head. 'Won't work, Flint,' he said harshly. 'I'm goin' to
kill you and that skulkin' brother of yours.'

'You're dead wrong, Condor. This is the end of the line
for you.' Still the other had made no move towards his gun
and it came to Frank at that moment that the other was
still stalling for time, waiting for Clay to get into position.
Just where was Clay? Frank knew instinctively that his life
could depend on him finding that out before Flint went
for his gun. Then, out of the corner of his eye, he saw the
sunlight glint off metal. In that instant, he knew where
Clay had posted himself, just inside the opening on the
top floor of the grain store where he could get an unim-
peded view of the street.

Another five seconds went by with all of eternity packed
into them. Then Flint Macey must have considered that
his brother was in position, for he went suddenly for his
gun, his right shoulder dipping downward, his arm sweeping across his body, taloned fingers a blur of speed. Even
before the other's hand had started on its downward

movement, Frank had thrown himself sideways, his gun out and firing while his body was still in midair, almost in a horizontal position. His first slug tore through Flint Macey's chest. For a moment, the other stood there with his knees buckling under him, a look of stupified amazement on his slowly slackening features. Even before his body had crashed into the dust, Frank's gun had belched smoke and flame again. The rifle bullet hummed viciously through the air where his chest had been a few seconds earlier, flattened itself on the ground behind his prone body and ricocheted along the street. The next moment, Clay Macey had lurched to his knees on the edge of the square opening, fingers clutching at his stomach, the blood trickling between his fingers and staining his shirt. He hung there for a moment, swaying, then pitched forward, his body turning in the air before he hit the ground, to lie still.

Frank stood up, automatically thrust fresh shells into his gun, then holstered it. Swinging round, he saw men appearing in the street, moving forward to stare down at the still bodies in the dirt, men who walked stiffly, their faces white with awe at this display of speed.

Frank walked past them, almost as if he did not see them. A few spoke to him, but he paid them no heed. Then he had reached the hotel. She was there, waiting patiently for him at the top of the steps.

'Are you all right?'

He went to her, led her inside. 'I'm all right,' he said then. 'The Macey brothers are dead. They made their play, and failed.'

'I'll get you some coffee, if you'd like that.'

'I think I'd like that almost better than anythin',' he said, smiling. For the first time. she noticed how warm his smile could be when it was not mixed with bitterness and sadness. Perhaps, in time, she thought to herself, she might be able to make him forget the trouble which had been haunting him for so long, and the thought of it was a growing warmth within her as she swept her glance suddenly up to him, then took his arm and led him into the dining-room.